LOVE AND MURDER IN SAVANNAH

THE SOUTHERN SLEUTH BOOK 1

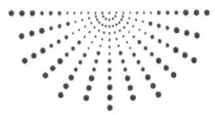

HARPER LIN

www.harperlin.com

PROLOGUE

SAVANNAH, GEORGIA, 1922

*B*ecky Mackenzie, at twenty-two, felt it was a good time to be alive. Her family owned one of the most successful tobacco plantations in the glorious South, and her life consisted of attending parties, dancing, and mortifying her poor mother by refusing to settle for any of the beaus Kitty Mackenzie was trying to saddle her with. Becky took to her father, Judge Mackenzie, not in looks but in speech. That was also a thorn in her mother's side.

"You are two peas in a pod," Kitty scolded Judge once, although it wasn't the first time.

"You say that like it's a bad thing," Judge replied with a sly smirk. "She has plenty of your traits, Kitty. That's why no matter how ornery the girl can be, the boys will always come calling. You don't think that concerns me as her father? You don't think I know what they're thinking about our baby girl?"

Becky had heard her mother's lecture on buckling up to land a husband a thousand times. Some of the ladies in the Auxiliary or down at the beauty salon or at any of the parties her parents attended would often ask when Becky would get married. None of them knew the meaning of minding their own potatoes.

Settling down when there was always a pair of strong arms to dance with or a wise-cracker to joke with or a handsome Northerner to get dizzy over was something only a jingle-brain would do. And Becky was no jingle-brain. She was a smart dame with a funny bone and no shortage of dance partners. Around her friends, she was said to be the bee's knees. And as if that wasn't enough, she had the uncanny ability to speak to the dead.

Yup, Becky Mackenzie was the cat's meow to the swingers and spirits alike. It wasn't until she touched a Ouija board at a birthday party that she realized flesh-and-blood people and dead-as-doorknob spirits had a lot more in common than not. They could be kind, or they could be deadly.

CHAPTER ONE

itty Mackenzie stood at the front door, looking out onto the long, winding driveway and shaking her head. She nervously patted the finger waves in her hair as if they could possibly come out of place. It was said by the ladies in town that buckshot could easily ricochet off her head because of the layers of setting lotion she used. But still, when she was nervous, Kitty patted her curls in place.

"Kitty, will you stop pacing the floor. The Heathcliff boy is long gone, and Becky missed him. Ain't no use fretting. I'm not all that fond of that boy anyway."

"Judge, that Heathcliff boy is a charming fellow, and he said that Becky told him to meet her here,"

Kitty replied to her husband. She turned around and glared at him sitting in the parlor with a book in his lap and a smoldering cigar in the ashtray next to him. "What will people think? She invites a suitor and then doesn't show up. It's poor manners."

Judge Mackenzie looked at his wife over round spectacles and furrowed his bushy eyebrows. More hair was on his face than on his head. He closed the book and folded his hands.

"Kitty, why are you so interested in marrying off our only daughter to anything in long trousers?" He picked up his cigar and took a puff. The smoke swirled around his head like a halo.

"That is not true, Judge. I just want her to start thinking seriously of her place in society. If she continues to act like she can climb trees and swim in the creek at her age without people talking about it, she's going to doom herself to the life of a spinster." Kitty wrung her hands and looked out the front door.

"You have a beautiful, intelligent daughter," Judge said as he set his book aside and then pushed himself up from his plush chair. "If you think you can pick her husband, I'm afraid you are going to doom your-self to a life without your daughter in it." He placed his hand gently on his wife's shoulder. "Besides, not all women want a milquetoast like that Heathcliff boy. Some ladies prefer a man with a little more fire in him." Judge's hand drifted down Kitty's back before he pinched her ample rump.

"Judge!" Kitty squealed, trying not to laugh. "You behave yourself! Talk about acting your age!"

"Excuse me, Miss Kitty. Mr. Judge. Dinner is ready." The deep voice came from behind them. When the Mackenzies turned around they saw the face of their butler, Moxley. He stood there in his white jacket buttoned all the way up to his neck and his black trousers pressed impeccably without a single stray hair or speck of dust.

"Thank you, Moxley," Judge replied.

"We should have invited the Heathcliff boy to stay for dinner." Kitty gasped as if she forgot to extinguish a candle in one of the barns where the dry tobacco was stored. "That girl's got my nerves so shot I'm no politer than a field hen."

"The last thing I want to see is that boy eating my food. He's so thin I'd see every bite slide down his spindly neck." Judge stepped aside to let his wife walk ahead of him. As she led the way to the dining room, she took his hand in hers as much out of affection as to prevent him from goosing her again.

"He's got a very nervous stomach. At least that is

what his mama told me. She says on account of him being born during a thunderstorm, he manages his stress differently." Kitty defended the poor Heathcliff boy as if he were kin. "But he is highly intelligent. I do believe if that daughter of ours would just give him a chance, she'd find him to be an excellent conversationalist."

"Because that is what all fathers want for their daughters. To find a man they can talk to," Judge replied as he held out his wife's chair for her.

"Oh, you are impossible." Kitty scooted in behind the table and looked at all the food on the table. "This looks lovely. I didn't realize it, but I am absolutely starved. All that worrying made my appetite blossom. Should we wait for—"

"No. Our daughter knows what time supper is. She can eat by herself in the kitchen if she can't arrive on time. I don't plan on letting Lucretia's fine fried chicken get a degree cooler." Judge folded his hands in front of him and bowed his head. Kitty did the same.

"Lord, thank you for this food and for all the blessings you've bestowed on the Mackenzie house. Amen."

For the first few moments in the dining room, the sound of clanking dishes and the scraping of forks was all that could be heard. With their plates filled, Kitty started talking first.

"Really, Judge. Do you think it would be wise to let our daughter just run wild? Look at what is happening here. She knows what time it is, and yet we are eating without her. She'll be in the kitchen like a servant, eating alone with cold food and no conversation."

"Serves her right."

"Oh, Judge."

"What do you want me to say, Kitty? On one hand, you want her to be adult enough to agree to the suitor of *your* choice, and on the other, you are worried she'll be eating a cold dinner alone in the kitchen," Judge said, smacking his lips before dragging a white linen napkin across his face. "Here's an idea, Kitty. Let her be."

Moxley chuckled but quickly coughed then cleared his throat.

"Fine," Kitty said. "I can see that you are more interested in contradicting me than coming to some sort of plan for our only child."

She took a sip of water.

"Now, you just calm down, Kitty. You're making a mountain out of a molehill. There ain't nothing for you to be fretting about," Judge said. "Now, can you let this man eat his meal in peace?"

"If we'd been proper hosts and asked that Heath-cliff boy to join us, I'm sure there'd be plenty to talk about," Kitty said defiantly.

"Do you think elaborating on his stomach problems constitutes proper talk for the supper table?" Judge snapped with a smirk. "I heard him going into great detail about the effect the Savannah River had on his delicate intestinal condition. You enjoyed that conversation?"

"I had asked him how he'd been. So, he told me."

Just then came a commotion in the kitchen.

"I done told you, Miss Becky, you can't come through the kitchen at suppertime!" Pots and pans clattered, making it sound like an army was charging through to the dining room. Within seconds, a smiling face appeared from the kitchen.

"Hi, Mama." A redheaded girl with skin as smooth as a Georgia peach and eyes as brown as dried tobacco strolled into the dining room from the kitchen. Her yellow afternoon dress was muddied around the knees, and her T-strap shoes were scuffed.

"My heavens, child, what have you been doing? Your dress is ruined." Kitty's daughter gave her a peck on the cheek, and then Kitty stared at her and gasped.

"It's not ruined, Mama." Becky Mackenzie smiled as she slipped behind her father and kissed him on top of his head. "It'll just need a few extra scrubs on the washboard. Oh my, this looks delicious."

Kitty folded her arms across her chest and pinched her lips. "You had a visitor today."

Becky pulled out her chair and took a seat as Moxley poured her some ice water. She smiled up at the butler, who gave her a quick wink. Within seconds her plate was filled with fried chicken, green beans, and biscuits the size of a pie tin. Within a few more seconds half of that plate was empty.

"That Heathcliff boy came calling. He said you told him to meet you here. You can imagine my embarrassment when you were nowhere to be found. Do you mind telling me where you've been all afternoon?" Kitty took a long drink of water.

"Are you sure you want to know, Mama?" Becky asked, her mouth full.

"Swallow your food before you speak. What were you, born in a barn?" Kitty said.

"Our Lord was born in a barn," Becky replied, dabbing the corners of her lips with her napkin.

"Don't you blaspheme, and don't look to your

father for approval of such comments. You are not too big to get soap in your mouth, young lady." Kitty huffed and took another sip of water.

"I'm sorry, Mama," Becky replied with a grin. "I was at the Old Brick Cemetery. Can you believe I found a stone from 1802? The rubbing came off beautifully. Would you like to see it?"

"Absolutely not!" Kitty gasped. In frustration she looked at Judge, who shrugged while he reached for the pecan pie that Moxley had just placed on the table. "Do you really mean to have me believe you'd rather spend time in that dirty old cemetery than with a gentleman caller?"

"If a gentleman came calling, I might have come home. But it was that Heathcliff boy. I'm surprised his mama's apron strings stretched so far." Becky turned to see her father choking as he attempted to stifle a laugh, causing the pecans to rush down the wrong pipe.

"Becky Madeline Mackenzie, I just don't know what to do with you." Kitty shook her head and pinched her lips together until they were white.

Watching her mother in such a state made Becky feel a twinge of remorse. She loved her parents dearly, and if they knew how hard she wished to make them happy, there would never be conversations like this one. But no matter how sincere her actions were, Becky always seemed to miss the mark.

Like today, she had every intention of coming home early. She'd been sent a rather juicy book from her best friend, Martha Bourdeaux of the Pooler Bourdeauxs, and was waiting for the right day to start it. A cloudy day with the chance of a storm would have been perfect reading weather. However, it turned out to be another warm sunny day that begged for a trip to the Old Brick Cemetery. It was peaceful there.

"Now I'll have to make reparations with Mrs. Heathcliff and apologize for my wild and ornery daughter," Kitty interrupted Becky's thoughts.

"No, Mama. I'll apologize myself. To be completely honest, I didn't know the Heathcliff boy was serious when he said he was going to pay a visit. He talks so crazy at times, like he just wants to hear himself make noise." Becky wiped the corners of her mouth and took a sip of water.

The Heathcliff boy had probably already forgotten that he'd even been at the Mackenzie plantation. The poor boy could be distracted faster than a cat, but if it would make her mother happy, Becky would make things right. Nothing was worse for a

Southern mother than to have other Southern mothers discussing her children's manners. She might as well have sewn a scarlet A on her chest. The scandal could be no less shocking.

If Becky had told her mother the truth that she had intentionally lost track of time to avoid Mr. Neville Heathcliff, her mother would have fainted from the scandal. It was a well-known fact among Becky's intimate circle of friends that the Heathcliff boy had a crush on her. At first, Becky had tried to be polite. She'd talk with him whenever he approached at the many parties they attended. She'd asked if he'd dance with her on more than one occasion but he had some constant condition that prevented him from cutting the rug. Of course, that wasn't enough to make Becky be downright rude to the fellow. She was sure he just didn't know how to dance and was too embarrassed to say so. But her aversion to him was something else.

One night, Becky had left a party. A friend of a friend of a friend who had a small shack on the edge of the city was celebrating…something. Things had started to get wild at about one in the morning, but before police could be called, Becky and a girl by the name of Susanna Something-or-other decided to scram. As they were walking home, their arms linked and they were still singing some of the songs they had danced to in the house. The moon peeked out from a stray patch of clouds. Had that not happened Becky was sure she would have never seen the Heathcliff boy—who was following them.

He hadn't spoken a word to Becky the entire night. She'd said hello and waved a few times but he responded with a blank stare. Another well-known fact was that the Heathcliff boy's mother had diagnosed him with several ailments that may or may not have been real. Mrs. Heathcliff told the women in town that her son often slipped into intense *thought sessions* where he'd just stare and stare. One ailment the Heathcliff boy confided in Becky was that *she* was the only woman he knew that didn't cause his nose to run or his throat to start to itch. When she laughed thinking this was a cute way to say he liked her, he intentionally knocked a glass to the ground. Then, he lapsed into one of those staring fits. Except he didn't stare straight ahead, he stared at her. His eyes followed her everywhere.

So after leaving the party, Becky and Susanna were shocked to see the Heathcliff boy since neither one had seen him slip out with them nor did they hear any footsteps.

"Getting out before the authorities show up?

That's a smart move Mr. Heathcliff." Susanna had said to him.

"Mr. Heathcliff, are you feeling all right?" Becky had asked hoping her voice didn't betray her nerves. Not to mention she hated the fact his first name never stuck in her memory.

"I'm going to…I'm…Oh no…" He clutched his stomach and darted down an alley.

"That poor boy is so smitten with you it makes him sick," Susanna said. She burst out laughing.

Becky snickered but her instinct told her to quicken her pace. It seemed like the streetlamps suddenly dimmed and everything became tomb quiet. She pulled Susanna by the crook of her arm, hurrying her down the sidewalk until they came to a busy street and caught a streetcar. All the while Becky kept looking over her shoulder. She didn't know what she expected to see. But something was coming up on her, she was sure of that. That odd feeling never left her whenever she saw Neville Heathcliff.

And now she had to see him. At least she'd be at home with her mother close by.

"I'll send for him tomorrow. I'll make sweet tea and cream cheese pound cake." Becky smiled, lifting her chin slightly as she searched her mother's face for approval.

"Girl, you don't know how to cook," Kitty needled.

"No. But Lucretia does. And I most certainly can mix up a batch of sweet tea as good as anyone in Savannah." She puffed her chest and watched her mother try not to smile. "Please tell me you forgive me, Mama. I'll make things right, and not only will you not have to endure the scathing stares of Mrs. Heathcliff, but you'll soon tire of telling her and the other mother hens out there that your daughter refuses to share her special recipe for sweet tea."

Kitty, although having firmer resolve than Judge when it came to Becky's discipline, couldn't help but let her anger and frustration melt away with her daughter's beautiful smile.

"I should take a hide to you." Kitty chuckled. "That boy would walk through Hades for you, gal. Isn't that worth something?"

"Daddy, you gonna stockpile all that pie, or can Mama and me have a slice?" Becky changed the subject and reached for the glass pie plate as her father was already helping himself to a second slice.

CHAPTER TWO

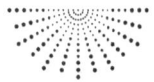

rue to her word and not wanting any more fuss with her mother, Becky retreated to her room to pen a note to the Heathcliff boy. As she leaned against the door and heard the comforting click of the latch sliding into place, she let out a deep breath.

For as long as Becky could remember, her room had been not just the place she kept all her special things but also her sanctuary. Her mother had allowed her to pick out the wallpaper when she turned sixteen, four years ago. Much to Kitty's dismay, Becky picked a robust maroon-colored paper that seemed more appropriate for a Gypsy fortune-teller's lair than a girl's bedroom. But since Kitty promised, it was what now covered the walls of her room. Pearl-colored lace curtains waved lazily as a warm breeze blew.

Having almost forgotten about the treasure in her pocket, Becky quickly went to her desk, sat down, and opened the thin side drawer. Inside was a stack of paper, bound together with a circular clip. Becky loved the crinkling sound the papers made when she shuffled through them. Carefully, she unfolded the paper from her pocket and spread it on the desk, trying to push some of the creases out with her hand.

"Napoleon Picard Bulloch 1732 – 1799. May you rest in peace, Napoleon," she said as she admired the tombstone etching before adding it to the stack of others.

The Old Brick Cemetery was just across the southern field, a mere thirty-minute walk from the Mackenzies' back porch. The cemetery had mesmerized Becky since she learned it was there. She was sure she'd covered every inch of the acres and acres of beautiful land dotted by hundreds of grave markers dating back to the War of Northern Aggression. As she grew older and developed a talent for drawing, she'd often take her sketchbook with her to the boneyard, where she'd study the mighty oaks draped with Spanish moss and the morning glories that grew wild among the headstones.

As the seed of rebellion that had been in Becky since she learned the word "no" really began to blossom in her teenage years, she'd often retreat to the cemetery to draw, write poems, or etch the oldest tombstones she could find.

Etching was something she'd read about in one of the many books her mother didn't know she studied. By placing a sheet of paper over the grave marker and rubbing her charcoal stub across it, the image of the engraving would pop right out. Even if the stone was worn down by the elements, the charcoal would pull it to the surface and allow it to be read as clearly as the broadsheets sold in town.

Napoleon Picard Bulloch was certainly one of the oldest Becky had come across, though Eugenia Ellen Evershade beat Mr. Bulloch by two years. She was laid to rest in 1730 after only living for two years.

Becky stared at the rubbings, admiring how each of the carvings was obviously done by a different hand. Some had short prayers of eternal rest included. Others had lists of family members. Some were simply the name of the dead and the years they lived. Becky wished to have a simple tombstone—no long list of relatives or sad words of death. Her headstone would be her full Christian name and her dates of birth and death. End of story. No fuss. Besides, who would ever come to visit her grave site besides maybe Martha? And she'd probably be too tipsy on mint juleps to know whether she was conversing with Becky's remains or Napoleon Picard Bulloch's.

The thought made her chuckle, and she made a note to relay the image to Martha when they next saw each other.

"No use putting it off, Beck," she said as she looked outside her window. "Get that letter to the Heathcliff boy done before Mama comes asking after it."

With a sigh, she pulled out a piece of beige stationery with the initials R. M. M. embossed in red at the bottom. She never liked the name Rebecca and insisted on being called Becky even as she was introduced at formal parties. It was just another quirk that drove her mother batty.

"Fine, here we go. Now, what is that Heathcliff boy's first name?"

She was stumped for a few minutes, trying to recall. While waiting for the name to pop in her head, she sorted a dish of pearl buttons, rearranged a handful of beautiful pebbles she'd collected near the creek, peeked through a glass kaleidoscope she'd received one birthday, and slipped out of her dirty yellow dress and into her green velvet evening dress with the dropped waist and plunging back, even though she had no idea whether her parents were expecting visitors or not.

"Oh, I give up. Dear Mr. Heathcliff." She decided the extra formality might make her sound all the more remorseful in her apology and prompt another visit.

"I am deeply sorry for missing you today. When you had indicated you were going to pay the Mackenzie Plantation a visit soon, I had no idea you meant today soon. I'd be so very pleased if you would come calling again tomorrow. In anticipation of your visit I am baking a cream cheese pound cake and making a fresh batch of sweet tea. I do hope you will accept my apology and join me on the front porch swing." She mushed her lips together because sitting with the Heathcliff boy on the swing was not anything she had any desire to do. But it would make her mama happy.

"Blah-blah-blah. Yours truly, Becky Mackenzie." Her face scrunched up as if she'd just sucked a raw lemon. Without giving the note another thought, she stuffed it in an envelope, rose from her desk, and went downstairs and into the kitchen.

"Lucretia, dear, can you bake me a cream cheese pound cake for a guest tomorrow?" Becky batted her eyes at the woman sitting across from Moxley at the small kitchen table. They were just finishing their dinner.

"I think I might be able to do that. Who's it for?" she whispered.

"The Heathcliff boy." Becky shrugged. Also at the table was a boy around seven years old. He wore his tight, curly hair close to his head, like his daddy, Moxley, did. His feet were almost always bare. Now was no exception.

"The Heathcliff boy?" Lucretia made the feeblest attempt at hiding her smile. "Didn't know you was sparkin' him."

"Oh, I'm not." Becky harrumphed. "I'm doing it for Mama. Teeter, I got a job for you."

"Yes, ma'am." The little boy turned to look at Becky, his eyes wide with excitement.

"When you are done with your dinner, will you deliver this note to the Heathcliffs' home? I'll have a brand-new shiny nickel for you when you get back."

"Yes, ma'am!" He squirmed in his seat and eagerly

gulped down his food, wiping his hands on his napkin.

"For heaven's sake, boy. Don't choke it down." Moxley chuckled as he rubbed Teeter's head. "I'll send him to you once he gets back, Miss Becky."

"Thanks, Moxley. You're top drawer. And thank you, Lucretia. I'll also be needing some sweet tea, but I think I can handle that," Becky said proudly.

"You do?" Lucretia asked, looking up at Becky from beneath long black lashes. "Miss Becky, I don't think you ever done so much as cut a tomato in my kitchen."

Becky pouted, put her hands on her lips, and looked up at the ceiling. "Fine. I'll leave you to make the sweet tea as well. But don't say I didn't offer."

"No, ma'am. I won't." Lucretia and Moxley both chuckled as they went back to their meal and watched Becky strut out of the kitchen.

With Teeter going to deliver the letter, Becky decided she needed to plan how to receive the Heathcliff boy as politely as possible and get him to leave as quickly as possible. It was going to be a rather daring episode.

Why can't it be Adam White paying a visit?

The thought had just popped into Becky's head unsolicited, forcing her cheeks to turn bright red and her mouth to dry up like a spring shower on the hood of her Daddy's Model T.

Adam White. Mama would never approve of him stopping by. Although his family was not poor in the traditional sense, they didn't meet the standards of the society folk in town. The Mackenzies had occupied this plantation for a hundred years. The Bourdeauxs of Pooler brought their wealth from Europe with them several decades ago. The Heathcliffs were in the railroad business. But the Whites were in newspapers.

Mr. White was a photoengraver on the printing presses in downtown Savannah. Adam worked alongside his father as an apprentice. The work wasn't glamorous. Every time she'd seen Adam, she couldn't help but notice the ink imbedded underneath his fingernails. But she never once thought less of him. In fact, it made her all the more interested in him.

"How marvelous it must be for you to see the news in print before the rest of us. You know all the happenings in the world before we're even out of bed," Becky stuttered one awkward evening when they ran into each other at a speakeasy she and Martha had snuck into.

Adam White towered at least a foot over Becky.

When he looked at her she was sure he knew every thought that went through her head, which made her blush all the more. She hated blushing.

"To me it's work. I don't really get a chance to read the stories. Once the papers come flying off those rollers, we've got to get them bundled and out the door. But that's all rather boring." He smiled and watched her cheeks turn red like she had some kind of fever.

As if his humble upbringing wasn't bad enough, Adam was a Yankee. His family had come to Savannah, Georgia, only a decade earlier. To the fine families around town, the Whites had no roots. Their lineage couldn't be traced, and even if it could, many old Southerners were convinced it probably went back to Abe Lincoln himself, and that was the same as having direct blood relations with Lucifer.

Still, Becky couldn't help where her heart wanted to lead her. As she went back to her room to finish getting ready for the evening, she took out her pocket sketchbook, the one she carried with her when she and Martha went to town. Becky flipped to a page marked with a pressed daisy.

On the page was a handsome young man with a square jaw. His hair was curly in the front and shaved fine and neat around the sides and back. His eyes were set wide beneath thick, pensive brows, and his lips parted only slightly when he smiled. She'd drawn this picture of Adam when he was across the room at the speakeasy. After she'd finished the sketch, he'd waved her over. She squeezed in next to him after he'd ordered his buddies to make room. He told her jokes and did funny impressions to make her laugh before getting serious. When she looked at him, she saw more than just a handsome young man. She saw someone who was waiting for adventure, for the unexpected to happen. Then he placed his hand over hers and squeezed it tight before letting go.

"It's Prohibition. We're breaking the law here," he said to Becky that night when they were sharing a drink.

"In more ways than one," she replied.

That memory sent tingles down her spine. She looked at the drawing of Adam. It was a fine rendition if she did say so herself. But as she looked at it again, the drawing seemed to shift. She blinked, then rubbed her eyes.

When she looked down at the sketch, it was no longer Adam but a strange-looking man, the type who would ride empty train cars and sleep in the open for years on end. Becky's heart pounded. She didn't draw this picture. She didn't know who this man was.

She rubbed her eyes again and the strange hobo was gone, once again replaced by the handsome face of Adam White.

Becky swallowed hard. She put her hand to her forehead. A fever might be a welcomed ailment since the Heathcliff boy couldn't arrive when she was feeling under the weather. But unfortunately, she didn't feel warm. Was it a trick of the light? Maybe her eyesight was going? Did she get enough sleep last night? Of course she didn't. She'd been out dancing as usual. That explained it. Becky was sure she was suffering from fatigue. It was nothing a good night's rest wouldn't cure. She would be sure to tell her entourage that staying out any later than one in the morning was out of the question.

Still, even as she tried to focus on her plans for the evening, the grimacing face of that dirty bum settled along the periphery of her mind.

CHAPTER THREE

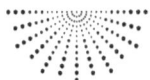

*A*fter eight that evening, the neighbors, the Rockdales, came over. Teddy Rockdale and Becky had been friends since childhood. Since Becky was an only child, she enjoyed the hoopla of the Rockdale home. Teddy was the same age as Becky but was smack dab in the middle of the family line-up. He had two older brothers, one older sister, and three sisters behind him while Mrs. Rockdale rocked the baby, Otis, in her arms.

"Why, Becky, you look as pretty as a picture. You meetin' someone special?" Mrs. Rockdale asked as she stroked the long ponytail of her youngest daughter, Emily, while the girl sat at the grand piano in the parlor.

"Just trying to impress your son, Mrs. Rockdale.

But I'm afraid I fall short," Becky teased as she nudged Teddy with her elbow. Everyone chuckled. Sure, the Mackenzies and the Rockdales would have loved to have their families joined through marriage, but it just wasn't a possibility. Becky and Teddy were like brother and sister. Nothing more.

"Are you ready to go?" Teddy asked.

"I am." Becky kissed her mother on the cheek and waved across the room to her father, who was enjoying mint juleps and cigars with Mr. Rockdale.

"Where are you taking my one and only child, Teddy?" Kitty asked casually.

"No place special, Mrs. Mackenzie. Just out and about. We'll be home early," Teddy said, following Becky's lead and kissing Kitty on the cheek before he and Becky left.

"You are in for a real treat, Becky. There's a juke joint right across the creek that's supposed to be jumpin'," Teddy said. "You feel like dancing?"

"Do I?" Becky clapped. "Oh, that sounds divine. I feel like I been cooped up all day in that house."

"I heard the Heathcliff boy came calling and you were nowhere to be found." Teddy looked at Becky from the driver's seat as he shifted the car into gear and pulled out onto the long driveway, heading toward the main street.

"Boy, that news travelled fast."

"Where were you, girl? You can tell me. You know I won't tell."

"I wasn't anywhere special." Becky smoothed out her skirt and stroked the beads on her purse with her gloved hand.

"You were at the cemetery. Don't try lying. I can tell by the look on your face." Teddy said.

"You know me too well." Becky clicked her tongue then smirked at her friend.

"So, did you see anyone there?" Teddy asked.

"The colonel was there. That poor man just can't seem to let go," Becky said as she looked at the countryside passing by. "I saw a robust woman I've never seen before. She looked me up and down like I just stumbled out of a tavern after closing time."

"Ha-ha. Did you talk to her?" Teddy asked.

"No. She looked busy. And a little scary." Becky bounced her eyebrows.

"They all sound scary to me," Teddy added. "And your parents still don't know anything about them?"

"Teddy, you know as well as me that if Judge and Kitty Mackenzie knew their only daughter could see the dead, they'd be as mortified as if I'd shown up naked at the Tybrisa Pavilion." She shifted in her seat as Teddy let out a whoop of laughter. "You did tell Martha where this juke joint is, right?"

"I didn't think you'd come if I didn't make sure your better half was going to be there," Teddy said as they pulled off the main road to a gravel road that quickly turned into a dirt path.

"You sure you know how to get there?" Becky asked.

"Girl, hush. You know if there's a swinging place to get some bathtub gin within a fifty-mile radius, I know how to get there." He polished his nails against his lapel.

"That, you do." She tousled his hair. "What a beautiful night."

Had anyone been eavesdropping on their conversation, Becky couldn't say who they'd fit for a straitjacket first: her for claiming to not just see ghosts but also communicate with them, or Teddy, who believed her.

Teddy had proven himself to be more than a trustworthy confidant. When she was a child and had her first encounter with a spirit, he was there. He saw nothing but Becky looking up at a rickety part of the fence that bordered the Old Brick Cemetery. She was carrying on a conversation with the broken and rusted spikes as if she was talking with any member of her family.

"What are you doing?" Teddy asked innocently.

"I'm talking with Mr. Wilcox. He says he's feeling better." Becky smiled her crooked grin. At the age of ten, she was as adventurous and brave as any boy in the neighborhood.

"Who is Mr. Wilcox?" Teddy looked around but saw no one.

"This is Mr. Wilcox, silly. Don't mind Teddy. He's a good egg," she said to the crumpled piece of fencing.

"Don't play games, Beck. It's rude," Teddy replied to her introduction.

"I'm not. Mr. Wilcox, this is my neighbor Teddy Rockdale. Teddy Rockdale, meet Mr. Wil..." Becky choked on the words because now she didn't see anything but Teddy and the rickety fence. "Well, dammit."

"Becky Mackenzie! Your mama would wash your mouth out with soap if she heard you cussing."

"Didn't you see him? He was a chubby man wearing overalls and gray jacket with shiny brass buttons." She put her hands on her hips. "He was right here."

"I didn't see no one, Beck. I just saw you carrying on a conversation with the fence," Teddy replied.

"But I'm not fibbin'," Becky insisted. She looked around. "He said his name was Mr. Wilcox. He said he hadn't seen a young 'un in a long time and that he was sure he'd never see Spanish moss again."

Teddy walked up to Becky's side. He looked closer at the broken bits of fence and wrapped his hands around the rusty bars and peeked over to the other side. Remnants of tombstones that had been broken and worn from years of exposure dotted the ground.

"Hey, Beck. Look at this." Teddy pointed through the bar to a tombstone just a few feet out of reach. "Am I reading that right?"

"I don't know. What's it say?"

"That looks like it says Robert Albert Wilcox." He kept pointing. "Right there."

Becky pressed her face against the bars, feeling the grit and dirt against her cheeks. She strained to see where Teddy was pointing.

"Well, I'll be. That sure does say Robert Albert Wilcox. What do you think it means?" Becky looked at Teddy.

"I don't know. Maybe you were talkin' to his ghost," Teddy said as if he were offering her a slice of apple pie. Over the years, as Becky became more and more aware of her unusual talent, Teddy never seemed to bat an eye.

"Why doesn't it bother me?" he had replied when she asked him this question at the age of twelve. "First, if it doesn't bother you, it shouldn't bother me. Second..." He laid his head playfully on her shoulder. "It's one of the many things that make you unique to everyone else I know. What good would it do me to tell everyone that you see spirits? They'd be convinced I turned to backwoods moonshine, and I'd be shipped off to the drunk tank for sure. No. I think your communications with those who have passed on is a secret best kept between friends."

~

*A*round a clump of trees, Becky saw a shack with strings of multicolored lights dangling from the drooping roof to a tall pole.

"We're here," Teddy said.

"This is it? It's nothing more than an oversized shanty." Becky sat straight in her seat. "I love it!"

The music that poured from the building came from a swinging live band. Voices of men laughing and women whooping could also be heard. The smell of cigarette smoke and gasoline overpowered the scent of the creek and the tall reeds that grew along the edge of the water. Other cars were parked at odd angles around the place, and a few bicycles lay lazily on the grass.

Teddy hopped out of the car and quickly got the door for Becky. After he offered her his elbow, the pair walked briskly to the entrance. A woman with smoky eyes and bright-red lips smiled as she ushered them in. The place was hot with bodies crammed tightly together, talking, dancing, or enjoying activities that required even closer contact.

"Becky! Over here!"

Becky's ears perked up at the sound of her own name. It didn't take but a second for her to see her dear friend Martha Bourdeaux waving her arms, kneeling on a chair at a small table surrounded by at least six people.

"Come, Teddy. Our adoring fans await."

"You go on, Becky. I'm going to get us a couple of drinks. Anything special I can get you?"

"Whatever is wettest," Becky replied with a shrug, kicking her heel up. She bustled over to Martha, who hopped out of her chair to give her friend a hug.

"What took you so long? I was afraid you weren't

coming." Martha huffed, taking Becky by the hand and pulling her toward an empty space where they could talk.

"Are you kidding? Why, I wouldn't have missed this for the world." Becky squeezed her friend's hand. "That's some band. Just those four fellows are making that music. Isn't it amazing? It sounds like Count Basie's got the whole gang here."

"I heard you left a poor gentleman caller waiting with bated breath at your doorstep. That Heathcliff boy was just heartbroken." Martha poked her friend in the shoulder.

"You heard about that already too? Teddy knew all about it as well." She jerked her chin in Teddy's direction as he approached holding a glass in each hand.

"A gin rickey for the lady. And how are you, darlin'?" Teddy leaned in to give Martha a peck on the cheek.

"I'm just fine, Teddy. I was asking our mutual friend here what happened with the Heathcliff boy. She was just about to tell me the gory details."

"I just plumb forgot. It isn't like the Heathcliff boy has that many qualities worth remembering." Becky took a sip of her drink. "I don't mean to talk so petty about the boy. It isn't his fault his mama hangs over him. But surely Mrs. Heathcliff has got to know we've nothing in common."

"You have plenty in common to a woman like Mrs. Heathcliff. You have lineage and land." Martha shook her head. "Nothing else matters."

"Well, it does to me." Becky took another sip. "Mama was dreadful angry with me too. She wasn't going to let her daughter make her the pariah of Savannah. I sent Teeter with a handwritten invitation for the Heathcliff boy to come calling tomorrow."

Again, Becky mushed her lips together as if she were being offered her least favorite food, liver.

"Well, bless your heart." Martha laughed. "You are a good daughter. The Heathcliff boy probably won't be able to sleep a wink tonight."

"Hey, I've a stellar idea. Why don't you and Teddy drop by? I'll pretend it's a big coincidence. Lucretia is making cream cheese pound cake and sweet tea. It'll be delightful. Plus, it would take some of the pressure off that poor Heathcliff boy. Lord only knows what nervousness does to his stomach and lower intestines. You'd be saving the man a heap of embarrassment."

"She is a smooth talker, isn't she?" Teddy nudged Martha.

"She sure is. I don't know, Teddy. She needs to learn her manners." Martha clicked her tongue before slipping her arm through Teddy's. "I think we'd better discuss it on the dance floor."

"You're going to leave me alone?" Becky pouted her red lips and put her hands on her hips.

"Oh, Becky, you won't be alone for long." Martha nodded, gave her best friend a wink, and hurried off, pulling Teddy along with her.

Becky took a sip of her Gin Rickey before turning around, and she was glad she did. She saw Adam White heading right for her. And there was no scary recluse leering at her. At least not that she could readily see.

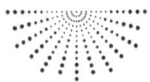

CHAPTER FOUR

*A*fter a few pleasantries, Adam whisked Becky out onto the dance floor. She felt as if she could have stayed on her feet with him until the sun came up. But when the band took a break, Adam took Becky by the hand.

"How about a little fresh air?" he asked. Becky nodded and looked at Martha, who was smoking a cigarette while watching. She winked at Becky then went back to the lively conversation at the tiny table.

Even though the night was warm, it felt downright chilly after emerging from the crowded shack. A shiver ran across Becky's shoulders, and she shuddered involuntarily.

"Are you cold? I can get my jacket from my car. It

smells like ink, but it's pretty clean." His smile took all the sense out of Becky's head.

"No. Thank you," she gushed, still holding his hand. "The cool air feels good."

They walked a little farther in the direction of the creek and the shadows of the trees, when Adam stopped.

"I'm glad I saw you here tonight," he said, looking up at the dark sky. "I've been wanting to ask you something."

"Oh? What is that?"

"I wanted to ask you if I might come ca—"

"Becky! Becky!" exclaimed Martha, charging out of the shanty. "We need you! Teddy's taken a turn!"

"What?" Becky asked with clenched teeth.

"I told him to slow down, but you know how he can get sometimes." Martha shook her head.

"No one can handle this? It has to be me?" Becky looked up at Adam with the biggest *I'm so sorry* in her eyes as she stomped toward Martha.

"I'm so sorry," Martha whispered then looked up at Adam and gave him a pleasant hello that he returned in kind.

When they were back in the juke joint, Teddy was in a chair, leaning against a wall and drenched in sweat with his eyes closed.

"Looks like it's time to go home," Becky muttered. "Can you kind gentlemen help me get my friend in the car?"

"I'll help you," Adam offered immediately. With one yank of Teddy's arm, he was over Adam's broad shoulder, being carried out like a sack of potatoes. Becky felt her knees turn rubbery as she saw Adam's biceps bulge. He carried Teddy like he was as light as a newborn baby. Once he had Teddy safely in the passenger seat, Adam turned to Becky.

"Oh, I can't thank you enough, Adam. And I had a wonderful time." She blinked her long brown lashes and smiled. "You're a very good dancer. Uh, what was it that you wanted to ask me?"

"It was nothing important," Adam said as he stood dangerously close to Becky, looking straight down his chest at her. "It can wait."

"But I don't know when I'll be out again. I mean, my family has all but booked my summer, and well, if there was something important you wanted to tell me, now might be the perfect time." Becky nervously fidgeted with the beads on her clutch.

"Well, it's a rather strange custom to someone like me, coming from up north, but I was hoping I could come and…"

"Becky? Can you take me home?" Martha

appeared out of nowhere. "Without you and Teddy, the night is basically over. May as well go home and count sheep."

Becky sighed and looked down at the ground. "Of course I can take you," she muttered.

"Thank goodness," Martha said as she climbed into the rumble seat. "Oh, this fresh air feels good. I'll never get the smell of cigarettes and gin rickeys out of my dress."

"I better be going, Adam," Becky said. "I'm sorry."

"Don't be. Savannah ain't that big a city." When Adam winked at Becky, she had to hold herself up with the open car door. Adam backed away, waving and smiling before disappearing inside the shanty.

"He is a really good-lookin' fella." Martha clicked her tongue. "For a Yankee."

"Martha, you couldn't have waited just five minutes to come get me? All I needed was five minutes. I'm sure he was going to ask to come calling on me."

"Why doesn't he just come calling?" Martha asked, tilting her head as Becky started the engine and put the car in gear.

"Have you forgotten Judge and Kitty? How would it be with a Yankee arriving at my door unannounced?" Becky shook her head. "No. My parents would need to be informed about Adam if he were to get a fair shake. And even then, I don't know if he would."

"Do you like him that much?" Martha asked.

"I don't know what it is about him. He makes me laugh, and he dances really well. But tell me, Martha, and be honest."

"Yes, he is Douglas Fairbanks and Rudolph Valentino rolled into one." Martha bit her lower lip. "I'm just being honest."

"That isn't what I was going to ask. Oh, I don't know what I'm saying. I'm so disoriented. I'm like a child lost at the zoo." Becky frowned as she looked at Teddy, who stirred slightly and then fell back asleep even as the car jostled him around.

After only having to backtrack twice along the dirt road, Becky found the gravel path that led to the main road and headed in the direction of Pooler, which was just on the outskirts of Savannah.

"Boy, it is a nice night." Martha tilted her head back, letting the wind tousle her brown hair. "It feels like we haven't been out together in ages."

"What are you talking about?" Becky chuckled. "We've seen each other at least once a week for the past two months."

"Yes, but we go out, and we find our fellas and

dance the night away and have so little time together. I think we need a good old-fashioned party." Martha's eyes popped as she leaned her head in between the two front seats.

"Oh, really? Could it be because someone's birthday is quickly approaching that the idea of a party is being suggested? I was born at night but not last night, Martha Olivia-May Bourdeaux," Becky said as she shifted gears.

"It'll be divine. We'll have a barbeque, and we'll move the furniture in the parlor for dancing. I'll invite everyone, and if you want to cause some scandal, I'll even invite your Mr. White." Martha batted her eyes. "He's a Yankee? Why, he was so chivalrous I would have never guessed it. Do I sound convincing? We'll just pretend we didn't know he was from the sinful dens of the North."

Becky laughed. "I think everyone in Savannah knows Adam White is a Yankee. No, that will get your party shut down faster than a goose on a June bug. Besides, I've only conversed with him on a handful of occasions. It's hardly an engagement."

The trio drove the rest of the way to Pooler with Martha doing most of the talking as she planned her upcoming birthday party.

"And charades! I love playing charades. We can

set up a card table for penny poker. This was your best idea ever, Becky," Martha said as Becky drove the car up the cobblestone drive that lead to the Bourdeaux Estate.

Unlike the Mackenzie plantation with its traditional white paint, wraparound porches on the first and second floors, and grand stoic pillars, the Bourdeaux Estate was a brick building that Becky always thought resembled a courthouse more than a home. But as she pulled up, a flood of wonderful memories of parties and barbeques and stories and secrets she had shared with Martha filled her head.

"In addition to me, who else will you be inviting to this grand event? Teddy should be on the mend by that time." She tickled her friend under the chin. His response was to grunt and slap her hand away without opening his eyes.

"We have to invite the Hershes and the McGowans, and I'm sure Cecil and June would be back from their trip." Martha pouted her lips, and her right eyebrow arched.

"What?" Becky asked suspiciously.

"I'll have to invite Fanny Doshoffer."

"Oh, why?"

"Now, I know your cousin is a hard pill to swallow, but—"

"Hard pill? She's arsenic," Becky argued. "That girl lives to aggravate me. Every single thing I do she's either already done or will be doing a thousand times better than me. I can't stand her."

"I know. But her mama and my mama are the dearest of friends. They have been since their families fought side by side in the Great War." Becky put her hand to her chest for dramatic effect.

"They were not in the Great World War together at all," Becky whined.

"I'm talking about the Civil War. What other war is there to a Southerner? Besides, she does often imbibe too much ambrosia. I find out all the juicy gossip about the people around town. Relations as well as strangers," Martha said as the car came to a stop.

"Lord only knows what that girl says about me," Becky replied, angrily jiggling the gearshift and yanking up the parking brake.

"Why, darlin', you know she does that only because she's jealous of you."

"Martha, you sound like my mother."

"Becky, in this instance she's right. Now, you go on and get this fox-trotting travesty home and then go buy yourself a new dress. I'll have the invitations in the mail by morning."

Martha hopped out of the rumble seat and gave Becky a tight hug and Teddy a peck on the cheek that he brushed away like a pesky fly. She kicked up her heels as she hurried up the steps to her house.

As Becky drove, her companion in the passenger seat at the moment was worthless in the art of conversation. So, without a second thought, she took a more scenic route back home that brought her past the official entrance of the Old Brick Cemetery.

With the moon showing half its face, there was just enough light for her to see by after she shut off the lights on the car. Before crossing the threshold of the boneyard, she listened. Teddy was snoring contentedly. The crickets chirped up a symphony. A barn owl screeched off in the distance. But other than that everything seemed to be asleep.

With her clutch under her arm and the pretty lace shawl she'd brought with her, Becky walked into the dark cemetery. The headstones stretched up from the dark shadows like crooked teeth. The oak trees that had grown to massive heights over decades reached high over her head as if they were trying to touch the stars.

Normal people would never visit the graveyard at this witching hour. Becky never once thought herself a witch. But she was looking to talk to someone.

Her heels made a *clonk, clonk, clonk* sound on the brick walkway that branched out in all directions. After making her way deeper into the heart of the cemetery, Becky found a long, flat above-ground tomb, on which she sat. The tomb was old and chipped around the corners, but the rest of it remained beautifully intact. It was too dark to read the name, but as Becky ran her hand over the letters, she felt a cool draft rush across her shoulder blades. When she turned her head to the right, she saw an older woman standing there.

"Good evening," Becky said with a smile. "Are you enjoying the night air?"

"I am," the woman replied. She wore a simple housedress like Becky had seen in family photos of her relatives who passed away long ago. "I've come to enjoy my strolls at this hour. So many interesting people out and about, like yourself."

She smiled pleasantly as she took a seat next to Becky. They chatted for a few moments until the woman abruptly stood up.

"Is everything all right?" Becky asked calmly. The behavior of spirits was sometimes unpredictable.

But up to this point, Becky had never worried about her own safety.

"Someone is watching," the woman said in a whisper.

"Someone...like you or someone like me?" Becky looked around in the darkness. She had never been scared in the cemetery even at the stroke of midnight. But something was setting her short hairs up.

"Neither," the woman replied before walking off into the darkness without making a sound.

"Neither? What does that mean?" Becky looked over her shoulder then straight ahead. She was just a couple of short minutes to the edge of the property. The sudden urge to be on her family's soil was over-powering. But once she was in the tobacco field, instead of feeling calmer, she sprinted to the back porch.

When she finally reached it, her hair sticking to her forehead and her shoes covered in dust, she looked behind her and saw nothing.

CHAPTER FIVE

rue to her word, Martha sent out invitations immediately. When Kitty entered the drawing room, she found her daughter casually sketching some of the new blooms that peeked from the flower box outside the window.

"Mail call," she said as she handed her daughter two envelopes. "Miss Martha is having a party for her birthday, I assume."

"She said she was going to send invitations immediately, and I'll swear she snuck out of her house in the middle of the night, barefoot and in her nightgown, to get these in the mailbox." Becky chuckled. When her mother didn't reply with a laugh or a gasp, Becky looked at her. "What's the matter?"

"I don't want any dramatic reactions to the other letter," Kitty replied, holding her chin high and her lips pursed. When Becky looked at the return address, she couldn't control her reaction.

"Fanny Doshoffer." She grimaced. "Oh, Mother, I can't." She held the envelope between her thumb and forefinger and tried to make Kitty take it back.

"What did I just say?" Kitty patted her finger waves. "Perhaps you'll be surprised by what she's got to say in that letter."

"Only if she's saying she's permanently moving to Africa to hunt lions. I'll be cheering for the lions." Becky muttered that last part under her breath.

"She's your cousin, Becky Madeline. And we will offer her every hospitality when she comes to stay with us." Kitty stared at her daughter.

"Comes to stay with us? Oh, Mama! She doesn't even like me. I'm female. If it doesn't wear trousers and have two cherries and a stem, Fanny isn't interested."

Kitty clutched her pearls and gasped.

"Why in the world would she want to come and stay with us?" Becky opened Martha's letter first and read in her beautiful script the date and time of the birthday party.

Immediately, Becky began to imagine what kind

of unique gift she'd get for her friend this year. She was turning twenty-one. Last year Becky found two halves of a robin's egg that she nestled into a small gift box padded with wild cotton. The year before that she found an exquisite piece of fool's gold that sparkled and shone almost like the real thing. She wrapped it in a cotton kerchief with the initial B stitched in the corner and fastened it with a blue velvet ribbon. Becky said to Martha that if she were to ever accept a proposal of marriage, she'd have her bring something blue.

"Becky? Are you listening to me?" Kitty insisted.

"Yes. No. What did you just say?" Becky stuttered.

"I said everyone in town will know she's coming. It will do you good to have some exposure to someone other than Teddy and Martha," Kitty repeated.

"What's wrong with Teddy and Martha?" Becky asked.

"There's nothing wrong with them, darlin', but the world is a big place, and a man wants to meet a girl with lots of interests and experiences. Not someone who repeats the same old dull stories."

"My stories about Martha and Teddy are anything but dull. Would you like to hear a couple? I've been saving them up for a special occasion."

"Becky, that sass is going to get you in deep one day," her mother scolded. "You are going to entertain your cousin Fanny and take her with you to Martha's party. She is anything but a stranger to the Bourdeauxs. In fact, you'd be wise to take a couple lessons from your cousin on the art of conversation."

"Conversation. Is that what they call throwing yourself at every man in the room? Okay. If you insist." Becky shimmied her shoulders.

"Your cousin Fanny is a respectable, refined young lady. People enjoy her company. I'll expect my one and only child to do whatever is in her power to make sure she has a memorable time with us."

Becky looked at her mother with more words dancing on the tip of her tongue just behind her teeth, which wanted to jump right out of her mouth.

What would her mother think of the conversation Becky had had with the woman in the cemetery, who had died of yellow fever only after she'd buried her husband and seven children? Or the young man who was hit by a train but stood next to his mama as she cried and cried watching his casket being lowered into the ground, unable to comfort her and tell her that he was not only whole again but happy and warm and safe? And there was her favorite, Mr. Wilcox, who told stories of his eleven grandchildren, his wife of thirty years, and all the jobs he had, starting when he was five, selling boutonnieres in front of the bank to the men working in the offices inside and ending when he was a wheelwright.

"All I'm saying is that you could learn a thing or two from Fanny," Kitty said before leaving the room.

"I could learn how to be an obnoxious pain in the—"

"I heard that!" Kitty shouted, making Becky wince.

She couldn't bear to read Fanny's letter in the house. Tucking her sketchbook under her arm, she marched through the house and headed out the back door, letting the screen slam shut behind her.

The heat of the day seemed to come down from the sun as well as up from the ground. It didn't help cool her temper either. By the time she made it to the cemetery, sweat pulled strands of her fiery red hair to her temples and across the back of her neck.

She found a quiet place underneath a massive oak tree. Beneath its canopy she immediately felt cooler. Without worry of being dainty or ladylike, she squatted down at the base of the trunk, ripped open Fanny's letter, and began to read.

Dear Cousin Rebecca,

I do hope my correspondence finds you well. I am

superb. Never in all my life would I ever have thought there would be a countryside more beautiful than Savannah, Georgia. But Granny Louise and I just returned from Europe. I do believe I've fallen in love with Paris. You would not believe the sights there. So many works of art and delicacies to eat, and I am so embarrassed that I had to turn down three marriage proposals on account that I could barely speak the language. The men are a good bit more forward than our Southern bucks. A girl has to keep her head. Your mother mentioned the Heathcliff boy had come calling on you. That's so cute. See, there is hope.

I will be staying at your family's quaint plantation in the upcoming weeks. Just in time for Martha Bourdeaux's birthday party. It isn't the kind of soiree I'm used to, but I'm sure it will be adorable. I've brought with me just the perfect gift I know Martha will love. She's never seen anything like it.

Looking forward to seeing you, cousin, and hearing all about your little hobbies.

Yours very truly,

Cousin Fanny

"Cousin Rebecca." Becky bit her lower lip until it stung. If she were to show the letter to her mother and point out all the veiled insults, Kitty would insist that Becky was being petty and maybe even jealous.

"I'm not jealous," Becky muttered. "Am I?"

She pulled out her sketchbook and began to doodle her thoughts as she searched her own heart for threads of jealousy where Fanny was concerned. After completing a rather off-color cartoon of her cousin getting a boot in the behind, she came to the conclusion that no, she was not jealous. Sure, Fanny was a lovely woman. She had strawberry-blond hair that hung in natural ringlets around her face. Her complexion was perfectly smooth without a single blemish or freckle. Every man with a pulse noticed her when she walked into a room. Granny Louise had placed all her money on that filly to win the derby, so Fanny had the finest clothes and read many books. How she could read so much and have nothing interesting to say was beyond Becky.

Just as Becky was about to leave the cemetery, she saw a familiar little figure approaching the entrance. It was Teeter. He knew too many of Becky's hiding places and was often sent by Kitty to find Becky and bring her back home.

"Hey, Teeter! What are you doing out here?" She waved, catching the little boy's attention.

"I'm just exploring!" he shouted back.

"Well, come on over here and sit a spell with me. Tell me what's new."

"Oh, no, ma'am!" Teeter shook his head. "I don't want no ghosts following me home! Mama says chi'ren who play in the boneyard get haunted."

Becky chuckled but didn't dare let him see her do so. The concerns of little children were no less serious than those of adults. At least, not in the children's eyes. So Becky stood, dusted off her dress, and with her sketchbook and letters tucked under her arm, went to join the little boy.

"Want to go walk through the creek?" Becky suggested.

"Yes, ma'am. It's powerful hot out here," Teeter said, taking Becky's hand as if she were nothing more than his lighter-skinned big sister.

"Yes, it is."

"What were you reading, Miss Becky?"

"Oh, a letter from Cousin Fanny. She'll be coming to stay with us in just a few days," Becky replied as if she'd just smelled something foul.

"Don't you like her?" Teeter asked.

"Not really. But the Lord gives us difficult people to help us reach Heaven."

Teeter screwed up his face as he looked up at Becky while still holding her hand. "Why don't the Lord give us easy people? Then we'd all get into Heaven."

Becky chuckled. "That's just not how it works. I'll race you to the creek."

"Ready. Set. Go!" Teeter cheated and took off running as Becky pretended to struggle down the hill to the cool, clear water. The water barely got over their knees at this end. Becky held up her skirt, and Teeter nearly drowned himself, splashing around, laughing, and gulping half the creek down his gullet. Still, his wide smile quickly made Becky forget about Fanny and her rude letter. Let her have Paris. Becky was more than happy right where she was.

CHAPTER SIX

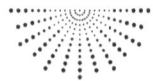

*W*hen Becky finally returned Teeter to his mama, they were both drenched, and their feet were caked with mud.

"Don't neither one of you think of coming in my kitchen with your feet like that. My goodness, Miss Becky, from the ankle down, you and I could be kin." Lucretia pursed her lips, shaking her head, and then chortled.

"We had some fun, didn't we, Teeter? It's too beautiful a day to stay inside the whole time." Becky poked Teeter in the ribs, making him giggle.

"I won't tell your mama you got the hem of your skirt torn." Lucretia pointed at the ragged fabric dragging behind her, which had been a lovely seashell color that morning but was now dark with water and mud. "If you can manage to skate past her without being seen."

Becky snatched the tea towel that hung from Lucretia's apron, quickly dried her feet, and began to tiptoe into the house. Lucretia chuckled again before turning to her son, who was falling asleep sitting on the porch step, his head lolling to the side against the railing.

Becky didn't know why she even tried since before she could reach the stairs her mother was there, her mouth hanging open and her hand to her throat.

"I can explain," Becky said, putting her hands out in front of her as if that might help calm her mother.

"Becky Madeline, what have you done to that dress?"

"It's quite all right, Mama. Lucretia already said she could fix it for me." Becky smiled, folding her hands daintily in front of her and peering up at her mother from beneath her long lashes.

"Your cousin Fanny cannot get here soon enough. Perhaps she'll have some kind of positive influence on you. There's got to be a lady some-where underneath all that mud," Kitty said worriedly.

Becky rolled her eyes and went upstairs to

change her clothes. Once in the privacy of her own room, she took off the dirty dress and flopped down in front of her vanity. She took out Martha's invitation and reread the details. The party was sure to be the social event of the season and hit on all sixes.

At the bottom of the invitation, Martha had included a tiny note in her elegant script that Becky had missed the first time. *With you in mind, I've arranged for some very interesting people to attend.*

"Oh, Martha. You wouldn't." She immediately thought of Adam White, and her heart began to race. "No. Mrs. Bourdeax would never allow a Yankee in her house. Or would she?"

The party was two weeks away. Martha had no idea what stress she'd put her friend under. One day, she would go no matter who was on the guest list. The next day, she would not go, coming down with a sudden case of the screaming meemies or a migraine.

She'd even turned Teddy down on four occasions to go out dancing.

"Since when did you become such a flat tire? Are you ill?" Teddy whined.

"No. I've got things to tend to. Besides, my cousin Fanny is coming any day now, and I have to make sure that everything is in order," Becky lied.

"Come on. Come with me. We'll cut a rug, and whatever is bothering you will be forgotten," he said, tilting his straw hat down and giving her an adorable grin while offering her his elbow.

"I can't, Teddy. But you'll be at Martha's party, correct?"

"Wouldn't miss it for the world," he said. "Next to you, she's my favorite Jane."

"Then when are you going to call on her right proper like a good Southern gentleman?" Becky asked. She nearly burst out laughing at poor Teddy's response. The poor man choked on words that refused to come out.

"Oh, calm yourself, Teddy. I won't tell," Becky flicked her finger under his chin. "But she's turning twenty-one. That's the perfect age for a set of hand-cuffs. I saw in the window of one of the jewelry stores in town that they had engagement rings. Have you bought anything for her yet?"

"Why don't you mind your potatoes?" Teddy blushed. "Has she ever said anything about me?"

"I'm sorry, Teddy, but I've got things to tend to here at the house. You have fun and throw back a few for me. Next time. I promise." Becky gave Teddy a peck on the cheek before seeing him out the door.

She'd seen a vision of Teddy and Martha. They

sort of passed by each other these days like people who passed each other on the sidewalk every day and slowly started to recognize one another until finally they were smiling and waving and looking forward to seeing each other for those brief few minutes.

That was something else Becky could add to her list of odd qualities. She'd never dare call herself a matchmaker, but she could definitely see who worked together and who didn't. Some people called it premonitions. Others called it a second sight.

There was no way to say whether this was a gift from her friends in the spirit world or if it was just because she paid attention. But Becky had learned long ago that most people missed the small stuff, whereas she found the most interesting things to be the obscure. It wasn't what the articles said that was so interesting but what they didn't say. And when people in town spoke, they often said much more than they realized.

Of course, this didn't apply to Becky's friends at the speakeasies and dance halls. They were there to drink and dance, and if any conversations took place, everyone was usually too out of breath to worry. Plus, there was a big difference between the crowd at the speakeasy and anyone putting on the high hat at Olson's Drug Store.

But Becky had sniffed out more than one cheating spouse without doing anything other than listening to them talk. On many occasions she kept her mouth closed only to see her suspicions confirmed as word reached her of a fella's clothes winding up in the middle of the street, tossed out by an infuriated wife. Sometimes she'd hear of a guy ending up in the hospital under suspicious circumstances when she knew he was on the lam for money to some palooka. And people would say things like, "Oh, he was such a quiet guy. Would always help out where he could." Yeah, so he could try to win back the money he lost on a nag in the sixth at Churchill Downs.

As she watched Teddy get into his car and disappear down the long drive, she was sorry she didn't suggest he pick up Martha. But then again, Martha was probably already at the joint, and they'd find each other.

Only after Teddy had been long gone did Becky wish she'd taken him up on his offer. The idea of a few drinks, some loud music, and a different dance partner for every step became more and more enticing. But then she'd remember Martha's cryptic words on her invitation, and the wet blanket would settle over her again.

Finally, the day of Martha's party came, and the weather had decided to muck up the works. It had been warm and sunny with that heavy Georgia heat for the past three weeks. But now as the sun was setting on the anniversary of the day Martha was born twenty-one years ago, the clouds decided to roll in and alter the blue sky to a dull, achy gray.

"I should have known," Becky said as her cousin Fanny arrived with the clouds. It was as if she brought the gloom with her on purpose.

"Becky! Get downstairs, girl, and receive your guest!" Kitty yelled from the bottom of the stairs.

Becky stood from her vanity, smoothed out her pale-blue skirt, and adjusted the rhinestone necklace at her throat before heading downstairs.

Fanny waited in the back seat of the car until the driver hopped out, dashed around the vehicle, and opened her door. The hat she wore added five extra inches to her height: it sported quail feathers and some berry-looking things.

"Aunt Kitty! Uncle Judge!" She smiled an almost perfect smile except for the gap between her front teeth. Aunt Kitty insisted it was charming.

"Oh, Fanny, you look as pretty as a picture!" Kitty

exclaimed as Fanny clutched her in a tight hug, rocking from side to side. "Why, Becky has been chattering nonstop since she got word you were coming."

"Why, who is that handsome beau coming my way? Is that Uncle Judge?"

"Girl, you know you didn't need to get all dolled up to visit kin." He patted her gently on the shoulder as she stretched up on tiptoe to give him a peck on the cheek.

"I knew for sure the most handsome men in all of Savannah were going be to here. I most certainly was going to dress to the nines." She batted her eyelashes.

As Becky descended the stairs, she felt her insides writhe and twist uncomfortably. This was torture. If only Fanny had arrived thirty or even twenty minutes later, Becky could have already been on her way to Martha's. But there was no use fussing about it now. For her mother, Becky cleared her throat, pulled her lips into a grin, and walked out onto the front porch.

"Is that Cousin Rebecca?" Fanny asked, putting her hand to her throat. "My heavens, Aunt Kitty. I never thought I'd see that day where Rebecca didn't have a stain or rip on her dress. Have you given up your tomboy ways?" she tittered as she walked up and wrapped her arms around Becky in an awkward hug.

"Not quite," Becky replied, smiling while crossing her eyes and looking at her father over Fanny's shoulder. He chuckled in reply. "I'll help you with your bags, Fanny. It's nice to see you. I think you'll be staying in the yellow room?" She looked at her mother for approval.

"Oh, no. Put her in the white room. That way she's right next to your room, Becky," Kitty instructed.

Becky nodded and picked up one of the satchels the driver had set on the porch steps.

"One more," Fanny said to Becky, pointing down at the second satchel, which was bigger than the first. With clenched teeth, Becky hoisted the bags up in her arms and headed inside while Kitty and Judge ran their mouths a mile a minute, with Fanny joining right in.

"Now you be sure to come down and have some sweet tea before y'all leave for the party," Kitty said as Becky headed up the stairs.

Becky bumped and rocked from side to side as each bag felt like it contained half a quarry.

The white room was a monument to Southern

femininity. Everything was pristine white. The lace curtains. The down comforter. The chaise lounge next to the French doors that led out onto the upstairs porch. The white was made even crisper by the dark color of the oak furniture.

"I've always loved this room," Fanny gushed as she entered behind Becky, who dropped the bags with a thud. "Rebecca, please be careful. Those bags must get me back to Paris someday."

"If they survived your boat trip, I think they'll survive me," Becky replied. "If you'll excuse me, I need to finish getting ready for Martha's party."

"Thank heavens," Fanny sighed. "For a moment I was afraid that was what you were wearing." Becky was about to reply when Fanny suddenly changed gears. "I have always loved this room. They'd never have anything so obscenely lacy in Paris, but it does have its own quaint charm."

"We should be leaving soon. Mama and Daddy are driving themselves. I'm sure you'd love to catch up with them. You and I will have plenty of time at the party," Becky insisted.

"Well, are you driving yourself?" Fanny asked.

"No. My friend, the neighbor boy, Teddy, is picking me up. He should be here any minute, and I still have to wrap Martha's gift." Becky saw the sudden interest in Fanny's eyes. They flickered like those of a wolf suddenly hearing the cry of a sheep separated from the flock. Every woman at Martha's party had better hold on to her beau tonight.

"Well, I'd just love to tag along. I'm sure your beau wouldn't mind," Fanny said coyly.

"He's not my beau. He's just… Teddy."

"Oh, you don't have to worry about me, Rebecca. I won't tell." Becky was sure she could trust the snake in the garden more than her cousin. "Does Martha know?"

"Know what?"

"That you are interested in this Teddy fellow."

"I'm not interested in him. He's just my friend. We've been friends for ages. Oh, but I think that you might enjoy the company of one of the fellas who I know will be in attendance. His name is… uh, the Heathcliff boy. His first name escapes me at the moment, but I'll bet you two will have a swinging time." Becky backed into her bedroom. "I just have to wrap Martha's gift."

"Well, if you need any help with your hair, give me a shout," Fanny said just before Becky closed her bedroom door. She walked over to her window and watched as the sky got darker. A little thunderstorm wouldn't stop Martha from having the biggest soiree in the county. She squinted as she looked across the tobacco fields toward the edge of the cemetery. It looked like the sky had cast a darker shadow there. Were her eyes playing tricks on her like they had been when the picture of Adam had changed? Yes, that was what it was. She just wasn't getting enough sleep. After Martha's party, Becky would hibernate like a bear for a couple of days.

Still, as she looked out the window, the dark shadow remained.

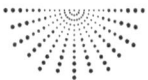

CHAPTER SEVEN

*A*s Becky listened to Fanny from the rumble seat of Teddy's car, she let her mind drift. As much as she'd like to bask in her distaste for her cousin and pick apart everything Fanny said with a fine-toothed comb, she couldn't concentrate on anything except those words in Martha's invitation. Who could she have invited?

"I'm telling you, Teddy, you'd be a natural in Paris," Fanny gushed.

"Thanks, doll, but I think I'll keep my feet right where they are. I think I might sound a bit like a rube with my Southern twang interfering with all that flowery dialect," Teddy replied.

"Nonsense. Wouldn't Teddy sound dapper speaking French, Rebecca?"

"Who's Rebecca?" Teddy asked.

"He'd be one dapper egg," Becky said before tickling his ear with the fingers of her gloves. He gave her a wink, clicking his tongue, then hit the gas, causing both girls to squeal with excitement.

"Goodness, will you look at this?" Teddy said as they neared the Bourdeaux property. Cars were lined up along the road, and dozens were parked in the grassy field leading up to the house. "I hope you ladies don't mind walking a piece."

"Not me." Becky pulled off her strappy evening shoes before hopping out of the car and swinging her purse over her shoulder.

"It looks like the Bourdeauxs invited the entire population of Savannah to Martha's party," Teddy said.

"I do hope you'll help make introductions," Fanny said as she wrapped what Becky would call her talons around Teddy's arm.

"Of course, Miss Fanny. But I do believe your reputation might have preceded you. Besides, you're like kin to Martha, ain't you?" Teddy asked.

"Our mothers have been the greatest of friends for years. But due to my traveling so much with Granny Louise, I've only just now gotten my bearings back here in Dixieland."

Becky could have fallen into a bottomless hole, and she was sure neither Teddy nor Fanny would have noticed if she did. But she had to admit she was quickly feeling the excitement mount as she hurried toward the house.

Lanterns along the grass lit a path to the front porch. As much as she wanted to be grumpy, Becky just couldn't. If Adam White was there, well, he was there, and so was she, and she'd dance with him and let him whisper in her ear, no matter what anyone thought of his Yankee upbringing. Besides, the war was long over.

A few fellas hung around the front of the house, smoking thick cigars, holding drinks in their hands, and clapping one another on the back as they told jokes and wove yarns. From inside she saw the shadows of couples cutting a rug as the music poured out of the open doors and windows.

Before she was discovered, Becky went wide around the house, straying off the lantern-lit path. The house looked like a wedding was going to happen there. Mrs. Bourdeaux had wildflower bouquets with lovely pink ribbons attached to every post around the place.

Without drawing any attention to herself, Becky walked toward the back door. Some people were there, too, but they'd retreated to the quieter end of the house to continue their conversations or even engage in a little necking. What was a party without a kiss or two?

"Hi, Becky," one woman said quietly as Becky climbed the back porch steps.

"Hi, Delilah. My, you look lovely. I love that color on you. Is that that handsome Zachary with you?"

"Hi, Becky." The fella standing dangerously close to Delilah smiled and tipped his straw hat.

Along the porch, long tails of pink crepe paper and curly ribbons dangled down from the ceiling. The kitchen was bustling as the servants chatted loudly with one another, pulling things out of the icebox and oven. The staff brought silver platters of delicious-looking dainties out to the guests and took empty silver platters to the kitchen at the same time.

Just as she was about to head into the house to find the guest of honor, Becky saw the birthday cake. It was a three-tiered beauty covered in white frosting and pink flowers. She walked up to it and locked eyes with Penelope, the Bourdeauxs' housekeeper.

"Don't you come nowhere near this he'yar cake, Miss Becky."

"I just wanted to take a peek, Penny," Becky said

as she innocently strolled closer to the counter where the cake was perched.

"Don't you dare. You goin' to stick you finger in my perfect frosting like you do all my cakes." Penelope pulled a dishrag from her apron and started to swat at Becky, who tried not to laugh.

"You always blame me, but it isn't me. Penny, would I lie to you?"

"Every chance you git. Now, go on! The party is in the other room and out in half the yard." Penelope swatted her with the dishrag.

But just as Becky was about to give up and leave, one of the servants collided with another, causing an empty silver platter and a full pot of water to crash to the floor, making a huge ruckus.

Becky made her move and gouged out a scoop of frosting with her index finger from the right corner of the cake.

"What in the name of Sam Hill are you two doing... Oh, Becky Mackenzie! I'm goin' to tell your mama!"

Becky hurried from the kitchen, smirking with her finger in her mouth as she waved to Penelope with the other hand. The big woman shook her head, but Becky knew she secretly loved it. Becky had seen Penelope's boy coming home from World

War I. After Penelope hadn't heard from him in over three months, she was sure he was dead. But Becky assured her he wasn't.

"He'll be wearing his uniform and looking as handsome as ever," Becky said soothingly. She couldn't bear to see Penelope so lost and sad. "You just trust me. You'll be seeing him within the month."

As with many of Becky's quiet predictions, this one also came true. Penelope's son arrived home safely.

"I've got to get a piece of that cake," Becky muttered as she slipped past a table full of men playing a serious game of cards.

"Hey, Becky. Pull up a chair. We could use another player," said one of them, winking at Becky as she squeezed past.

When she looked down at the guy shuffling the deck, she recognized him from a couple of places Teddy had taken her to. His name was Tim or Tom. Something with a T, she was sure of that. He shuffled the cards until they were a blur. When he looked up at Becky, it was obvious from the glaze over his eyes that he'd had quite a few drinks. Becky smirked as she looked down at the cards. A yellow-eyed devil looked back at her as she watched each card slide in front of the men.

"Ha. So you can take my money, Pete? I ought to tell your mama you're trying to lure me into this game of sin. Even got Beelzebub on the suit." She laughed. "Save me a seat. I'll be back."

All the men chuckled except the dealer, who watched Becky as if he were seeing what her dress covered. As the weight of his gaze got heavier, Becky quickly walked into the first door on her right that led right into the study. She was going to exit through one of the open French doors that led to the porch but froze in her tracks.

There in the corner, staring up at the shelves of books, was that Heathcliff boy. With about as much grace and subtlety as an English bulldog in a bed of tulips, Becky ran to the door and quickly made her getaway in the direction of the front of the house. Sure, she was behaving rather rudely to the Heathcliff boy, but she'd make it up to him later.

"Becky Mackenzie!" called a familiar voice from the corner of the porch where a small group of people had gathered.

Becky squinted then smiled when she recognized the full figure of Aunt Rue. She waved and sauntered along the porch, finally slipping her shoes back on.

Aunt Rue wasn't really an aunt of Martha's. She was a woman from town whom everyone called

Aunt Rue. She was very wealthy but for all intents and purposes looked like she just stumbled into town, perhaps falling out of an open train car door or shuffling up some dusty back road. But she was the kindest heart anyone ever could meet and was holding up a tall glass of something to Becky.

"What is this?" Becky asked.

"No matter. Take a sip."

Becky did as Aunt Rue ordered, and her eyes bugged.

"Yikes. That hooch will peel the paint off the walls." Becky handed the tall glass back to Aunt Rue. "Is Martha's mother serving that?"

"No. I brought my own," Aunt Rue said, pulling a slender flask from her robust bosom. "Let me know if you want a snort."

"I think that swig will do me the rest of the night," Becky replied.

"Good. I never did like sharing. But the real reason I wanted to call you over was to thank you." Aunt Rue linked her arm through Becky's and led her into the house. It was at least ten degrees warmer inside, but Becky didn't mind. "Thank you for John."

"You don't have to thank me, Aunt Rue."

"I do. I had myself all in knots over that man. I

was sure he'd taken up with some Sheba and that was why he was sneaking around all the time. You have to believe me when I tell you he was acting a mite out of sorts."

Aunt Rue pulled an elaborate black lace fan from the other side of her bosom and began to fan her sweaty face. John, who she fretted over like a mother hen over a chick, was her gardener. Some people suspected he did more than tend her magnolias, but Becky knew better. They were the best of friends, like brother and sister. But there had been a rift that Aunt Rue was sure had something to do with some harlot trying to steal John from her. For his gardening ability, of course. Aunt Rue had won the blue ribbon for her flowers from the Home Garden Club of Savannah for the past seven years. She wasn't about to give up that title just so John could have a woman.

"So, who was the person he was seeing?" Becky asked.

"A friend of his from the war had stumbled into town. Hard on his luck. Nowhere to go and suffering from the shakes. John had put him up in the cellar without my knowledge. Like I'd have tossed an American soldier out on his ear." She shook her head and pinched her lips together. "Aunt

Rue is a lot of things, but heartless ain't one of them."

"Have you both squared things away?" Becky asked. She waved to several familiar faces and searched for Martha as Aunt Rue bent her ear.

"We have." Aunt Rue squinted at Becky. "How did you know? Did you follow John? Did you spy on him?"

"Aunt Rue, sometimes it just takes a keen eye and a little distance to see what someone else is missing." Becky couldn't very well tell her that the spirits she spoke with gave her the skinny on half the town. "I'm just glad it worked out for you."

"Mitsy Hamilton was right about you."

Becky shivered at the name Mitsy Hamilton.

Mitsy had asked Becky for similar assistance as Aunt Rue. But the conclusion was at the opposite end of the spectrum. Becky told her she'd find the truth in her barn, which was nothing more than a small, dirty unused shack that was home for a few cats and some spiders. At least, that was what Mitsy thought. When she found Mr. Hamilton in that dirty, cramped shed with her best friend, well, Mitsy Hamilton was ready to hang them both from the nearest tree. It was only the other woman's screaming that saved them. Becky had almost sworn off peering into the spectral plane for answers to questions about cheating spouses. Had Mitsy succeeded, Becky would have turned herself in as an accomplice. She could not have lived with the guilt. But who would believe her?

Fortunately, Mr. Hamilton and his mistress escaped the wrath of Mitsy by the skin of their teeth. Rumor had it they were somewhere in Tennessee, penniless and miserable, or so Mitsy was telling people.

"Mitsy Hamilton knew all along. She just needed someone to confide in. That's all." Becky finally spotted Martha, but Aunt Rue held her arm tightly.

"You can weave that yarn, Becky Mackenzie, but some of us see that there is more to you than meets the eye." Aunt Rue smiled while her right eyebrow arched up her broad forehead. "Don't worry. Your secrets are safe with us."

She winked and finally let Becky's arm go. With a blush and a shake of her head, Becky squeezed Aunt Rue's hand.

"Take it easy on that hooch, Aunt Rue."

"I'll take it any way I can get it." She raised her glass, took another sip, and gasped as she let it take her breath away before turning back to the group she'd left on the front porch.

"What was Aunt Rue chewing your ear off about?" Martha asked as she latched on to Becky tightly.

"Oh, you know. Old ladies like to ramble to anyone who will listen. Something about a shed and some rope. I don't know. She's lit," Becky fibbed.

"Good. It's about time you join her." Martha pulled Becky through the crowd to the bar, where a good amount of liquor of varying colors in multitudes of jars, bottles, and barrels was on display. "Here, try this. Daddy got it from a fellow pulling a wagon down the back roads just this morning."

"Is this what Aunt Rue is drinking? Because I'm already daffy after a sip of her poison," Becky muttered.

"Where's Fanny?"

"Bringing up the rear with Teddy," Becky replied.

"That didn't take long," Martha replied before tossing back the last of whatever was in her glass. "Can you believe all these people?"

"Funny thing is I know just about all of them since they are your kin. My goodness, is there ever a party that they don't come to?" Becky teased as she smoothed Martha's brown hair and tucked a couple of stray strands behind her friend's ear. "I love how they never seem to change. Like Tallulah." Becky pointed at a hefty woman laughing while she sat at the picnic table in the backyard.

"What about my Aunt Tallulah?" Martha started to laugh.

"I've known her for my entire twenty years of life, and she never had a different hairdo," Becky said. "And Cousin Billy. He's been wearing the same suit to every family reunion regardless of the fact that the buttons are ready to burst under the strain."

"Becky, you are too much," Martha said, still laughing.

"And look, sister-woman Fiona from the church."

"She sings in the choir with Mama," Martha said.

"She cries at every party. Not even a drop of liquor in her, and look, she's bawling now." Becky put her hands on her hips and clicked her tongue.

"Well, I've got a real surprise for you. Come on. I want you to meet some people." A devious grin spread over Martha's lips.

"Who?" Becky stood still. "Who did you invite? Your invitation said you specifically invited interesting people for me to meet. Who is it? Did you invite Adam White? I'll just die if you did."

Martha stopped, looked her friend in the eye, and smirked. "So you've really got it bad for that Yankee. I'm sorry, Beck. I didn't extend an invitation to the strapping young man, but I will make sure to do so at the next gathering."

"Don't bother." Becky shrugged. "I'm sure I can find someone just as good to cut a rug tonight. Besides, I don't know if that big palooka would have fit in your foyer. He's built like a sand barge. Probably just as bright. Did you ever notice he doesn't speak much? There's nothing worse than a fella who can't carry a conversation. Nothing worse." She batted her lashes, smiling happily.

Deep down Becky was disappointed the Yankee wouldn't be there.

"My mother would have strung me up, birthday or not, and given me a pop in the chops if I invited that Yankee into her home." Martha shook her head, her brown curls flopping across her face. "She's probably gushing over Fanny as we speak, since the girl is the perfect specimen of a Southern belle."

"It's okay. When you said special... well, I just never know what to expect from you, Martha."

It didn't take long for the regular gang to share a drink or a quick dance with Becky as she and Martha strolled through the house. Out on the back balcony was a cluster of rather dramatic figures.

"These are my special guests," Martha said, squeezing Becky's hand in hers. "Hold on to your hat. These folks are the bee's knees. I can't believe my mother, Mrs. Bourdeaux, agreed to having them attend."

Becky studied the guests Martha was pointing out. At first, she thought she saw a rather solemn crowd around them. Then she realized there was no crowd. Not of living people, anyway.

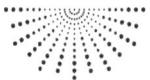

CHAPTER EIGHT

"*B*ecky, I want you to meet Madame Cecelia and her escort, Count Ernesto," Martha said with her chin high and her eyes twinkling. "They are going to provide us with the entertainment this evening. You and Teddy arrived just in time."

As soon as Becky looked into Madame Cecelia's eyes, she felt the strange sensation that every secret she had was on display. The happy piano and clarinet music coming from the phonograph that had half the house stomping on the floor had suddenly become mute, as if Becky were hearing it with cotton wedged in her ears.

"Miss Becky, I have heard so much about you." Madame Cecelia's eyes were green jewels peering out from several layers of smoky black liner. Her full lashes fluttered hypnotically up and down. She had red lips that matched her nail polish. Every few seconds, she took a deep drag from a cigarette perched in a long black holder with rhinestones around the tip. Small black wisps of hair clung to her forehead from beneath an elaborate turban that sported a purple gem in the middle. She was draped in a similar purple shawl with fringe that nearly reached the floor.

"Madame Cecelia is going to read our palms and tell our fortunes. Isn't that a gas?" Martha clapped.

"I'd love to take a look at your palm, Miss Becky. I bet you have plenty of stories to tell." Madame Cecelia smiled while she looked down her nose slightly, the black eyebrows she'd drawn in arching dramatically. "Don't worry. You needn't say a word. I'll know it all in just one glance."

Becky nodded slowly as she studied the woman. She had plenty of creases across her forehead and around her eyes when she smiled.

"And what is your specialty?" Becky turned to Count Ernesto.

He tipped his tall black top hat before stroking his pointed goatee and adjusting the cuffs of his shirt. His fingers were the longest Becky had ever seen and reminded her of a spider's legs.

"I have a few tricks up my sleeve," he said with a heavy Cajun drawl while pulling a long-stemmed rose from behind Becky's ear.

"Aren't they too much?" Martha giggled. "I couldn't wait for you to meet them. I thought this would be so much fun." Just then Martha heard her name being called. "Who bellows?" she called back. "I'd better go and check. I'll be back in a jiffy." Martha hurried off, only to be swept up in the Charleston by a handsome man whom Becky had seen many times before. His name was Ralph, if she remembered correctly.

"Becky, I was told you possess some very interesting skills. Would you care to elaborate? Birds of a feather, you know," Madame Cecelia said as she blew smoke from the side of her mouth.

"I'd rather have a drink," Becky replied.

"You don't have to be afraid of us here," Madame Cecelia said, nodding toward Count Ernesto. "Any of us. It's those creatures that linger where we are most comfortable that are more dangerous."

"Well, there you are." Just then Fanny horned her way into the group. "I swear, I got snagged for a dance and then another and another. I just needed to pull away for a moment to catch my breath." She batted her eyes at Count Ernesto. He wasn't a particularly handsome man, but he *was* a man, so that was good enough for Fanny. Becky made the introductions but could not pull away quick enough.

"You know, I was told while I was in Paris that I had certain psychic qualities. Granny Louise and I had attended a party where there was a Gypsy fortuneteller. She was quite taken with me, I must say. She said my aura was stronger than anyone's she'd ever encountered. The aura is the energy field around every living thing, you know. I've always felt extremely sensitive to people's energies."

"Is that so?" Madame Cecelia asked, nodding as she looked at Fanny then Becky and back again.

Becky caught Madame Cecelia's eye. Did she think Fanny was as full of hot air as she did?

"Yes. I just know what a person is feeling, or I can sense where something has happened or if something is going to happen. I don't know where it comes from. I'm just special, I guess," Fanny tittered, pulling her shoulders up and swiveling her hips.

"Well, why don't we take a look? Let me see your dominant hand." Madame Cecelia took Fanny's hand. She traced the creases in her skin while tilting her head this way and that, her red lips drawn down.

She muttered something quietly before gently pulling Fanny's fingers wide.

"I see the ocean. You travelled a great distance recently." Madame Cecelia watched Fanny's expression.

"Yes, I spent the last few months in Paris."

Becky rolled her eyes. Not only was this feeding into Fanny's already inflated ego, but who didn't know she was just back from Paris? Fanny made sure she said as much every five minutes.

"You left in a hurry," Madame Cecelia said.

"Well, we'd already stayed so long, and I was getting homesick." Fanny winked at Becky.

"No. There was another reason. A woman was looking for you."

Fanny coughed. "I beg your pardon?"

"A woman. She was very angry."

"I don't know anything about an angry woman in Paris," Fanny stuttered.

"No. Not in Paris. In Brussels. You travelled to several cities in Europe, no?"

Madame Cecelia had struck a nerve. As much as Becky would have loved to hear what this was all about and why an angry woman in Brussels was looking for Fanny, she felt a twinge of guilt for enjoying the spectacle. Still, she didn't look away.

"There was a man. Handsome fellow," Madame Cecelia said before Fanny yanked her hand away.

"I'm not sure what you think you are accomplishing, Madame Cecelia, but we spent only a brief time in Brussels. Hardly enough time to unpack. To be quite honest, I don't think this is a proper discussion to be had in mixed company." Fanny rubbed her hand against her skirt as if there were germs on it.

All of a sudden, the music stopped, and there were cheers of hip-hip-hurrah for Martha on her birthday.

"I believe Miss Martha is going to open her presents." Fanny clapped. "I can't wait until she sees what I picked up for her in Paris." She narrowed her eyes at Madame Cecelia and Count Ernesto as if daring them to say another word.

Within seconds, she slunk away, grabbing the attention of every man in the house. Teddy, who had been leaning against the fireplace, quickly grabbed a fresh cocktail and trotted up to her, offering the vamp a cool drink.

"That one is an ultra-maroon," Madame Cecelia said.

"You said a mouthful," Becky replied.

"Becky, I'd really enjoy it if you could come to my

home for a visit. Coffee perhaps." Madame Cecelia smiled. "I do believe we have quite a bit in common."

"Maybe." Becky was not used to strangers inviting her into their homes for coffee. She grew up knowing almost everyone in Savannah, living and dead. But Madame Cecelia and Count Ernesto were not locals. She might be a fakeloo artist who lured gullible women into her parlor while he rolled them for cash. Just because the madame managed to spot the holes in Fanny's Paris stories didn't mean she was any kind of real psychic. Had Becky the patience or interest, she probably would have picked up on the same details the fortune-teller did. That was how they worked. They'd pick out a patsy, find out all they could about that person behind their back, then spout the facts back at them as if they'd been delivered from a mountain. This was more or less some kind of flimflam.

"It's not a trick," Madame Cecelia replied, making Becky's cheeks burn. "Unlike your friend, I didn't get my psychic abilities from some frog in Paris."

Becky couldn't help it and chuckled at Madame Cecelia's comment. The flamboyant older woman seemed to be the only person who was on to Fanny's ruse. Becky had no choice but to like her. Still, she wasn't sure how she felt about someone she just met knowing about her own special talents. If she were willing to air Fanny's dirty laundry, who was to say she wouldn't drop the dime on Becky too?

Just as Becky was about to walk away, Madame Cecelia grabbed her hand. She didn't squeeze it, but Becky couldn't pull her hand away without making a small scene. She looked into the woman's eyes while squaring her shoulders. One thing Becky Mackenzie wasn't afraid of was putting a person in their place if need be.

"Things are about to change for you, Becky. Don't fight it." As quickly as she took Becky's hand, Madame Cecelia let go.

"What does that mean?" Becky smirked.

"You've got the trust of many people in this room. Your special gifts have worked well for you *and* them. But every coin has two sides. For every kindness, there is a cruelty that feels it was robbed of its chance."

"Look, I know this shtick gets you invited to a lot of posh parties, but I'm not some yokel who fell off the turnip truck. I don't know what you are hinting at. But people who can't be clear when speaking can't be trusted."

"She's a sharp one," Count Ernesto muttered before mingling in with a group of ladies heading inside. He pulled scarves and flowers from all angles, making the ladies gasp and clap. He did something that resulted in a shower of golden glitter before he and his entourage stepped out of view. Becky hated to admit it, but she was rather impressed with his skill. It was all an illusion, of course. A sleight of the hand. Nothing more.

"But no, Becky. It really is so much more." Madame Cecelia arched her eyebrows again. "Tonight is where your journey begins. Where it will take you, I don't know. But I hope eventually it might be to my doorstep. I'm right next to a very old apothecary that would probably have more than one or two things of interest to you, a kindred spirit being just one of them."

As much as she wanted to be skeptical, Becky found herself smiling. She liked Madame Cecelia if for no other reason than her willingness to be so brazenly different from everyone else.

"Would you like your palm read? Perhaps you'd rather see what the cards have to say?" she asked, sweeping her hand to a tiny table in the corner of the porch with a candle glowing eerily in its center and a deck of tarot cards next to it.

"I think I'd rather go join the poker game I saw going on inside. Depending on who's dealing, those cards might be saying a little more to me." Becky winked, but before she turned her back, Madame Cecelia started to laugh. It was a pleasant sound from deep in the fortune-teller's belly. Hearing it made Becky smile.

As Becky made her way to the dining room, where all the guests had gathered to watch Martha open her presents, she decided she might just call on that weird palm-reader when all this was over. Any excuse to drive into town was good enough.

Just then, Penelope, with the other servants in tow, came slowly treading into the dining room with the birthday cake lit like the Chicago Fire.

"Happy birthday to you!" she started, and then everyone joined in. The cake was big enough to feed at least fifty people, and if there weren't that many in the house, the number was darn near close.

Martha sat still as the cake was presented to her. She looked over the candles and zeroed in on the small but noticeable indentation made by someone's finger.

While looking over the room, Becky saw Teddy beside Martha. They were chatting and nagging each other like normal, making Becky feel better. The last thing she wanted for her best friends was for Fanny to butt in. Leaning against the fireplace was Pete,

Teddy's friend. He looked well lit. There was Margo Something-or-other wearing a lovely light-blue dress with black lace over it. Her skin was shiny with sweat, since she'd been dancing the whole night. There were some relatives of Martha's that Becky had seen at other parties, as well as a couple of dapper gents she'd seen at a few shanties.

And then Becky's heart lodged in her throat. Approaching her from the other side of the room, bumping into as many people as possible in the process, was that Heathcliff boy.

Becky was trapped. She couldn't leave and miss Martha opening her gifts. She quickly put on her most convincing smile and extended her hand to him.

"I saw you come in, Miss Becky, but I hadn't a chance to talk to you," the Heathcliff boy said as he pushed his glasses up the bridge of his nose and smiled down at her.

"That Martha stole me away lickety-split. You know there's no telling that girl anything, especially when it is her special day. So how are you..." Still, his first name had yet to rise out of the murkiness of her memory.

"I was a little concerned this morning that I

might not be able to make it to this evening's festivities." He rubbed his stomach.

"Same problems?" Becky asked, hoping not to get too many details.

"Yes. Mother wanted me to stay home. She said, 'Neville, the heat of that house and the smoke will most certainly aggravate your condition.' But I haven't had the urge to use the bathroom since I got here," the Heathcliff boy said proudly.

"Who is Neville?" Becky asked.

"Oh, um… that's me. Neville Alexander Heathcliff."

Becky cleared her throat. "What did you get Martha?"

"Hmmm? Oh, her gift." He leaned in close to Becky's ear. "A thermometer."

"Practical yet thoughtful. I like it." Becky had to admit it was a clever gift. And her approval appeared to send a shock wave of satisfaction through the young man.

"What about you?" The Heathcliff boy braced his arm against the wall over Becky's right shoulder, putting his other hand on his hip. He reminded her of Mr. Peanut, except he had spectacles and not a monocle. But that was the only difference she could think of immediately.

Without saying a word, she pointed at Martha, who had picked up the elegant little box. Becky had slipped it on the table without being noticed before Martha had grabbed her hand and led her through the house.

"Becky Mackenzie, where are you, girl?" Martha squinted and batted her lashes as she saw the Heathcliff boy towering over her. "There you are, hiding. I wonder what this could be."

Becky had wrapped the small box in two sheets of the thinnest brown paper she could find. It crackled beautifully and was slightly waxy to the touch. She'd bound it with a yellow ribbon that she knew would find its way into Martha's hair sooner or later. She watched her friend open the tiny box and stared.

"Becky, it's beautiful." She pulled out a long silver chain that had a perfectly round piece of magnifying glass set in a marquisate frame.

She didn't dare tell Martha it was one of the many trinkets she'd found in the cemetery. If Becky had to guess, she was sure it belonged to one of the ladies from a plot in the northwestern corner. There were many Old Colony names there, and Becky could envision some ripe old dame with her waist cinched in an uncomfortable corset and wearing a hat with two-foot-tall feathers, this piece of simple but elegant jewelry, and half a dozen strands of pearls.

Martha slipped it over her head immediately. "I just love it." She put her hand over her chest. Martha was a little tipsy, but Becky knew her feelings were genuine.

"Martha! Open mine next!" Fanny called. For a few precious moments, Becky had forgotten her cousin was there. "I brought it all the way from Paris."

"Oh, brother." Becky sighed.

"That was a lovely gift you gave Martha," the Heathcliff boy said. "Very thoughtful. You are a very thoughtful person, Rebecca Mackenzie. Can I get you another drink?"

I'm so thoughtful I can't remember your first name, and you just said it one minute ago. "I'd love a drink. Something wet," Becky replied, waiting for the Heathcliff boy to chuckle, but her silly joke went right over his head.

Fanny had pulled up a chair right next to Martha, squeezing in dangerously close to Teddy while at the same time making goo-goo eyes at Pete.

Martha took the box from Fanny. It was wrapped in elegant paper with a unique paisley print on it.

Becky was sure she got it in Paris. She almost blurted that out as she giggled at her own joke but decided not to say a word. Martha tore the paper with reckless abandon, and her eyes bugged.

"It's pronounced 'wee-jee board.' Isn't that just the most elegant spelling?" Fanny asked as she took the box from Martha. She opened it up and placed the board in front of the guest of honor.

"Now, when I was in Paris, I went and spoke with a bona fide Gypsy fortune teller. She had one of these here boards and said she talked to spirits all the time!" Fanny exclaimed, evidently relishing having all eyes on her. "You lay the board on a flat surface. Then you lay your fingers delicately on this piece called the planchette."

"Oh, let's play it now!" Martha squealed, clapping her hands. "Becky! Come sit next to me."

Just then the Heathcliff boy returned with a mint julep in each hand.

"I hope one of those is for me," Becky teased.

"Of course it is. I offered to get you a drink. The other one is for myself," he replied seriously.

Becky shook her head. "You go on, Martha. I'll catch the next round." She watched as Fanny quickly took control and grabbed ahold of Teddy, Pete, and another fellow who looked like he had some mischievous ideas in his head. He had a glazed, feverish look in his eyes as he studied Martha and Fanny. Obviously, he just had too much to drink. Or maybe he was up to something.

"Now, I was told by the old Gypsy that I have a very sensitive aura, so I will lead the spirit board. It's a way to communicate with... the dead. Everyone, place your fingers on the planchette." The entire group gathered around the table did as Fanny instructed while the rest of the guests around the room watched.

"You don't believe in all this stuff, do you?" the Heathcliff boy asked.

Becky shrugged. She certainly didn't believe Fanny could conjure up anything other than a severe case of flatulence. But she watched as Fanny rolled her head and shoulders as everyone kept their fingers on the heart-shaped planchette.

"Spirits hear me," Fanny called. "If there is anyone on the spectral plane, we are ready to hear you. Talk to me. Can you hear me?"

Nothing happened.

"I am reaching out to the realm of spirits. Can you hear me? Anyone wanting to communicate with us still in this earthly realm, we seek your knowledge. Can you hear me?"

Still nothing.

"Spirits, do not be afraid. We seek answers to the afterlife. Can you hear me?"

"I think I know some spirits that will answer a heck of a lot quicker," the glassy-eyed man said. "Hey, Hank. Pour me another drink and crank up that Victrola."

The entire room roared with laughter. For a split second, Becky felt bad for Fanny, who looked deflated that her psychic ability wasn't strong enough to keep the audience interested. But before she felt too sorry for her, Becky observed Fanny grab Teddy's hand and yank him to the dance floor in the parlor, leaving Martha just sitting there.

"Uh, er... honey, be a dear and go get Martha one of those delicious mint juleps," Becky said to the Heathcliff boy. "I'm going to help her cut the cake."

The Heathcliff boy smiled and tittered at being called "honey" and headed toward the bar in the parlor.

"Did you see that?" Martha asked Becky. "I haven't even danced with Teddy yet. I always get a dance with Teddy."

"I did. It was your decision to invite her. I could have told you she'd have her mitts on just about every single fella here. Makes me glad you didn't invite Adam White."

"Don't say that too loud, or the Heathcliff boy might overhear you."

"What a wet blanket. The only one Fanny didn't make doe eyes at," Becky grumbled. "I'll bet my mother told her to back off the Heathcliff boy. He's the only caller coming to the house."

"He comes from a very good family. Do you think it would be so horrible to consider…"

"Martha, bite your tongue." Becky looked around. "Where is the Heathcliff boy? I swear I just told him to go and get you a drink."

Just then, some glass broke, and a huge roar of laughter echoed through the house. "Good heavens, someone let in some barnyard animals. Wait here, Beck. I'll be right back, and you and I can try this game."

Martha slipped from behind the table and went into the other room. Becky looked down at the board. The letters of the alphabet were written on it as well as the words "yes" and "no." With her lips pouted as though she were thinking, Becky reached out, and without her hand touching anything, the planchette slid beneath her fingers.

The first thought that came to her was about

Adam White. Before she could ask anything, she envisioned his handsome face and broad shoulders and the dimples in his cheeks. Did he have feelings for her? Were they real feelings or the kind that came with too much drinking and dancing? Would her parents ever approve of her seeing a Yankee?

Before she could ask a question, she heard a scream. Not a party scream. Not the kind of scream a woman would let out when she was having fun. But a terrified scream that went on and on until it became pitiful gasps.

Becky bolted out of the dining room and hurried in the direction of all the commotion. There she found Fanny, as white as a ghost. Her entire body shook as she stared at the floor. At her feet was the body of Lawrence Hoolihan with a knife sticking out of his back. The knife still had birthday cake frosting smeared on it.

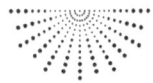

CHAPTER NINE

"I can't believe it," Judge said as he drove Becky and Fanny home. Teddy insisted on staying with Martha, much to Fanny's dismay. Whether someone was murdered or not, she had expected him to escort her back to the Mackenzie Plantation.

"Poor Lawrence Hoolihan. Poor Martha." Kitty shook her head. "It's going to be all over town, if it isn't already. What are people going to think?"

"Some are going to think she throws one hell of a party," Becky chortled.

"Bite your tongue, young lady." Kitty turned and looked over her shoulder at her daughter in the back seat. "I don't know the Hoolihans, but I'm sure they'll be just torn to pieces."

"Lawrence Hoolihan was known at quite a few speakeasies. He was a good dancer when his hands stayed put." Becky watched her mother clutch her pearls.

"I just can't believe I was telling that man all about Paris just a few short minutes prior to the whole horrible event," Fanny blubbered. "He seemed so interested. Such a gentleman."

"I wouldn't go that far," Becky harrumphed.

"Rebecca, that is a cruel thing to say. The poor man is dead." Fanny fanned her face with her hand.

"I knew that *gentleman*. I'm not saying he deserved to die. I'm just saying what he said and what he did were two very different things." Becky looked at Fanny. "You just might be singing a different tune had he continued to drink and got you alone."

"Becky, that's quite enough," her father grumbled.

"Not everyone is a saint when they die, Daddy."

"Oh, I've heard enough." Kitty shifted in her seat. "I don't want to hear another word about this horrible incident."

"I wouldn't be surprised if those two scoundrels dressed like Gypsies had a hand in all this tragedy," Fanny insisted, ignoring Kitty's desire to change the subject. "They were shifty."

"They were the entertainment hired to do parlor tricks," Becky said, wanting to defend the strangers. As much as she didn't like it, she couldn't help but hear Madame Cecelia's words echoing in her head. *Kindred spirits.*

"They were strangers who looked desperate and dirty," Fanny insisted.

"That isn't true. What did your fortune-tellers in Paris look like? Probably not a whole lot different. Just because something has a French accent doesn't automatically make it highbrow."

Fanny pinched her lips together and glared at Becky. "Rebecca, I don't expect you to understand since you've never left Savannah, but the world has all kinds of people in it. You learn to recognize the bad apples when you travel."

"I don't need to travel to know a bad apple when I see one." Becky glared until her mother cleared her throat and inserted herself in the conflict.

"Oh, this terrible night has taken its toll on all of us," Kitty said, reaching back and patting Fanny's knee while giving her daughter a stern look. "We don't need to argue with each other. It is a matter for the police now. Poor Martha. Her birthday will be forever marked by this gruesome event. She's the one we should be thinking about."

Becky had to agree with her mother. Poor Martha. She would be the topic of conversation all over Savannah and Pooler. But as Fanny and Kitty droned on about helping the Bourdeauxs with some homemade chicken soup and corn bread, Becky went through the long list of characters who were at the party. There was a murderer among them.

~

The next day, Becky woke up early despite the slight pounding in her head. She blamed Aunt Rue for that. Whatever that woman had been drinking could probably have started a fleet of bi-wings and enabled them to cross the Pacific.

After drinking the glass of water on her nightstand, Becky shook the cotton out of her head and quietly got cleaned up and dressed. She wanted to get back to Martha's house without anyone suggesting she drag Fanny with her.

"Drastic times call for drastic measures," she muttered as she tiptoed out onto the balcony.

The sun was up, and the only noise came from the kitchen, where Moxley and Lucretia bustled about, preparing breakfast. The smell of coffee was too much for Becky to resist. While hiking her dress up dangerously high, she swung her leg over the railing and hooked her foot in the trellis, which was covered with ivy. Slowly, she made her way down. When her feet finally hit the ground, she realized she'd torn her nylons. They sagged and made her legs look droopy.

"I'll get another pair from Martha," she muttered as she stepped into the kitchen from the outside.

"Miss Becky," Lucretia whispered through clenched teeth. "Are you just getting in? Your mama will skin you alive if she finds out that—"

"No. I wish I had that much fun last night," Becky said as she took a seat at the small kitchen table. "I'm going back to Miss Martha's. She had an awful time last night, and I just want to check with her. I was hoping I might get a cup of coffee for the journey."

Lucretia watched as Becky batted her eyelashes, frowning slightly like the poor soul hadn't a friend in the world. After rolling her eyes, Lucretia placed a delicate cup in front of Becky with the strong, black, steaming liquid inside. Becky sighed after the first sip.

"That'll cure what ails you." She leaned back in her chair and touched the snag in her stockings.

"You're not going to wait for Miss Fanny to wake up?" Lucretia asked, looking sideways at Becky.

"Well, if I wanted to wait for half the day to pass, I would. That heifer sleeps until noon. No. I'm going to see Martha on my own, and I'll probably be back just before she wakes up." Becky took another sip.

"You aren't planning on walking all the way to Pooler, are you?" Moxley asked. "It's going to be powerful hot out there."

"Nope. I'm walking all the way to Teddy's and letting him drive me."

Becky watched Lucretia pull a flat pan of corn bread out of the oven. It smelled so good it made her stomach grumble. Before she could ask Lucretia to sneak her a slice, the woman set the pan down, gouged out a steaming hot square, slipped it into a tea towel with little flowers stitched on it, and handed it to Becky.

"You'd best get going. Your father will be up now that the cornbread is done." Lucretia snickered and turned her back to continue cutting the squares of cornbread.

Becky took the golden bread gratefully and, on tiptoe, kissed Lucretia on the cheek.

"You're a swell egg, Lulu," she said as she headed toward the door. Moxley smiled and waved as she stepped outside, careful not to let the screen door bang.

"Hey, Miss Becky!" Teeter called from his seat on the porch. His mama didn't allow him underfoot in the kitchen when she was cooking breakfast.

"Hey, Teeter." She walked over and broke off a couple of crumbs and handed them to the boy. Within seconds, they were gone.

"Bye, Miss Becky!"

Becky waved and hurried along the well-worn path that led to the Rockdale property. And just like Teeter, she ate the rest of the cornbread, then she licked her fingers clean before wiping them on the tea towel. It was a splendid time of morning. The birds chirped wildly, and the air was warm but hadn't yet decided to become oppressive and weighty and pull all the desire to have fun right out of a person. The wet strands of tall grass tickled across her calves as she ventured off the path to snag a couple of yellow wildflowers growing along the way. The stems were still wet with dew. The grass smelled strong and clean.

Off in the distance, she could already see the Rockdale home. It was a grand place that had been in the Rockdales' family just as long as the Mackenzie plantation had been in her family. If a cross word ever transpired between the two families, it was dead and buried with the folks who did the speaking, because they'd been like kin for so long.

When Becky came into view, Teddy's father, who wore a seersucker suit and a straw hat, was busy telling one of his hired hands what was wrong with one of his tractors.

"I'm convinced it's the belt. You know how my machines purr when they run." Mr. Rockdale pointed deep inside the belly of the red machine. "You'll have to get deep in there, Lionel. But mark my words, it's the belt."

"Yes, sir, Mr. Rockdale," Lionel replied without a pinch of hesitation.

"Why, good morning, Becky." Mr. Rockdale beamed. "I heard you all had quite a bit of excitement at the Bourdeaux place last night."

"You heard right," Becky said as she gave the round man a peck on the cheek. "I was hoping Teddy was home. He did make it back, didn't he?"

"I'll say. And I had quite a few words for him leaving you and that pretty Fanny to find another way home. I didn't raise that boy to be such a knave."

Becky chuckled at how Mr. Rockdale's sentence came out. "It was all right, Mr. Rockdale. My parents were there. We got home just as safe as you please.

Besides, I think Teddy wanted to stay to comfort Martha. That is what a gentleman would do."

"Oh." Mr. Rockdale pulled his lips down at the corners and nodded. "I didn't realize. Well, the old boy is up having his coffee on the back porch. You know the way." Mr. Rockdale waved and went back to studying his tractor's guts. "I'm telling you, Lionel. Just check the belt."

Sure enough, Teddy was exactly where his father said he would be. Sounds came from his house, but then again, with all the children and constant flow of family and friends visiting, Becky couldn't remember a time when the house wasn't noisy.

"Well, look what the cat dragged in," Teddy said, squinting while shielding his eyes as he looked in Becky's direction.

"You look awful," Becky said. "Good thing Fanny isn't here, or she might find you too distasteful for her tales of French adventures."

"Very funny."

"Come on. Get that coffee down your gullet and come with me to Martha's house." Becky stood with her hand on her hip.

"Those are some nice stockings. Is that a new style?"

"I had to climb down the side of the house to get

here without waking up the house," Becky said as if she were saying nothing more than what a beautiful morning it was.

Teddy screwed up his face.

"To put it the way your daddy did, I didn't want to drag a pretty Fanny along with me." She shrugged, and Teddy chuckled.

"I'm sorry, Becky. I can't go to Martha's like this. I stayed with her until almost three in the morning." Teddy yawned. "I'd be absolutely worthless to her and you, and my head is pounding."

"But Teddy, how am I going to get there? You know my parents won't let me take the car after... that incident." Becky flushed red.

"You mean to tell me your parents haven't forgiven you yet for—"

"No, they haven't, and I don't want to talk about it." What Becky had done or failed to do with her father's car was a topic Becky refused to entertain. Only Teddy and Martha knew what she'd done, and they were sworn to secrecy.

"Well, I'm not thinking straight this morning. My brains are trying to escape from my skull. So, here." He pulled his car keys from his pocket. "You can use my car. Just do me a favor and bring it back—"

"In one piece. I get it." Becky grumbled as she

snatched the keys from his hand. "Thanks." Reluctantly, she kissed Teddy on the top of the head, making him wince but also smile. Within minutes, she was driving down the long dirt road off the Rockdale property, heading toward Pooler and her dearest friend.

CHAPTER TEN

"I didn't sleep a wink," Martha said as she took a seat on the porch swing next to Becky. They'd done that since they were little girls. How many secrets and stories of theirs that the swing had eavesdropped on was a mystery. "Mother is beside herself. The police only just left when the sun was coming up. We had to give them the name and address and physical description of every one of my relatives. Do you know how long that took?"

"Obviously until almost sunrise," Becky replied.

"Do you know how awkward that was? Cousin Mavis has those warts. And Ginny Lynn has that eye that goes off on its own. It was horrible. Mother kept giving me dirty looks just for telling the truth." Martha sighed. "I'm exhausted."

"Do they have any idea who might have done it?" Becky leaned forward.

"If they do, they didn't say anything to us. They crossed half of us off their list because we were occupied while it was committed. But that still leaves about a dozen blokes. I sure hope they corner whoever it was quickly." Martha looked down and pointed. "What happened to your stockings? You get jumped on the way here?"

"I wish. No. So I'm guessing you aren't interested in coming with me into town?" Becky hoped her friend had a little left in the tank.

"Normally I'd love a chance to get away, but I'm too tired. Plus, one thing I know about the people in this Southern paradise is that they love some good gossip. I'm used to being the one spreading it, Becky, not the topic of it." She frowned, her eyes filling with tears.

"It'll be fine, Martha. You know in a week or two someone will do something much more scandalous than this, and you'll be all but forgotten," she said soothingly. "Why, I can just hear it now. That Martha Bourdeaux thought she had it bad with a man being murdered at her twenty-first birthday party. Not compared to so-and-so who is going to have so-and-so's baby out of wedlock while so-and-so's mother is in the nut house and their father is in the nearest gutter."

"You sure do know how to make a girl feel good." Martha wrinkled her nose. "Besides, I promised Mother I'd help her clean up. Thankfully the police didn't notice the gin in the bathtub."

"Don't kid yourself. They did. And if I know your father, he offered them a snort or two that they gladly accepted." Becky sniffed and straightened her back. "You don't think those coppers have red noses because of the cold temperatures."

"You are probably right."

"I know I am." Becky smiled as she stood up and extended her hands to help Martha out of the swing. "And I'm in no hurry, so I'll help you clean up."

"Oh, I was hoping you'd say that. I'm just dreading going into the house and into the hallway by the study where the body was." Martha clicked her tongue. "I only invited Lawrence because he was Pete's friend. I didn't know him all that well, but he seemed nice enough. A little grabby at times, but I've been guilty of that too."

In a short time, Becky swept what seemed like fifty pounds of streamers, confetti, bits of broken glass, and cigarette ashes into a pile just outside the back door.

"You are a good friend, Becky!" Leona Bourdeaux, Martha's mother, exclaimed. "This whole incident has got me so worried about my baby girl." She stroked Martha's hair, making Martha roll her eyes.

"Mother, you do carry on."

"Just you wait until you have children of your own. Then you'll understand the continuous apprehension I've felt since the day I brought you home from the hospital. My beautiful baby girl."

Leona was a thin woman who often acted the damsel in distress around her children. However, Becky had witnessed on one occasion when Leona had lost her temper with a foul-mouthed rummy down on Baker Street.

Leona had taken the girls out for ice cream on a hot summer day when they were just at that awkward stage of leaving childhood and becoming young ladies. Ice cream was still good, but walking with Mother holding their hands was not.

So, Leona walked a few paces in front of the girls, far enough to let the feeling of independence wash over them but close enough to hear them talking, when a man stumbled out from an alley and made the kind of remark only a drunk would dare say to a lady. And Leona Bourdeaux was a lady. Her brown hair was swept neatly from her face. Her dress was stylish and impeccably pressed, and the seams in her stockings were as straight as arrows.

What that man said, Becky didn't know. But it made Leona gasp, stare in disbelief, then haul off and slap sobriety right into the fellow. He staggered back, lost his footing, and landed solidly on his rump.

"You'll get worse than that if you ever speak like that to me again!" she shouted as she adjusted her skirt, then she patted her hair in place, took the girls by the hands, and stomped off, muttering the whole way about the sad state of chivalry.

When it came to Martha, she doted on her. But Martha knew better than to ever intentionally upset her. Like Becky, Martha didn't just love her mother but respected her as the woman of the house. Of course, she still rolled her eyes at the woman when she got all wishy-washy.

As Martha and her mother stacked the dozens of empty glasses on silver trays and handed them to Penelope in the kitchen, Becky strolled slowly and carefully down the hallway where the body was found.

There was still a trace of blood on the floor where Lawrence Hoolihan had fallen. Becky crouched down and studied the stain. Just then, a chill raced down her spine, and she heard a voice.

"I didn't know."

Becky immediately stood up and looked around. She was the only one in this part of the house. Mr. Bourdeaux was outside still. No other men were in the vicinity, but she was sure the voice was male. Swallowing what felt like dust in her mouth, Becky stepped over the threshold between the hallway and the vestibule that led to the parlor.

Just a few hours ago, there had been a folding table right there and a couple of gents playing poker. People had danced all around them. How could someone have killed a man without being noticed? As Becky walked around, she spotted something on the floor between one of Leona's lovely display cabinets and a bookshelf. It was one of the playing cards with the devilish face on it.

"How did this get here?" Becky asked. Were the card to fall from someone's pocket or from their hand, they would have had to hide between these two pieces of furniture. The culprit would have been standing there waiting to ambush poor Lawrence.

Before anyone noticed her, she tucked the card into her brassiere. For a second, it felt like it would freeze her skin. But as quickly as it chilled her, the cold receded, and she went about finishing her sweeping, keeping her thoughts to herself.

"Well, Becky, I'm sure your mama needs you at home to entertain Fanny," Leona said, making Martha chuckle as she stood behind and to the left of her mother. "You two gals don't be strangers. Martha is in need of a nap, but she'll be as right as rain come evening time. You come back, and I'll have some sweet tea or lemonade for you both."

"That sounds real nice, Miss Leona. I can't promise, but we will do our best to stop back." Becky ground her teeth as she watched Martha giggling.

Leona nodded and left the room to check on Penelope and the other servants as they were polishing the silver, washing and drying the dishes, and preparing lunch.

"You be sure to bring Fanny back now," Martha tittered as she slipped her arm through Becky's, linking them at the elbow.

"You don't ever want me to come back, do you?" Becky shook her head.

"Of course I do." Martha squeezed her arm. "How are things with Fanny so far? Are they what you expected?"

"Worse. And she's taken a shine to Teddy."

"She has?" Suddenly Martha had something else to worry about. "Is Teddy interested?"

Becky could hear the nervousness in Martha's voice. Fanny had all the right parts in all the right places. Worse, she knew it too. Rare or blind was the man who didn't pay any attention to her when she walked into a room.

"You know Teddy. He flirts with anything in a skirt." Becky tried to squash Martha's worries. "Besides, she isn't staying here. She's just here for a couple of months. Less if I have any say in it."

Martha took a deep breath and looked out the front door.

"Don't worry," Becky insisted. "You are every bit as pretty as Fanny and better than that, you've got a sense of humor. I wouldn't worry about Teddy if I were you."

"Well, why would I? It isn't like he has made any commitment to me officially." She rolled her eyes. "Besides, I'm the talk of the town. People are just dying to come to my parties."

"Truer words were never spoken." Becky kissed Martha on the cheek and promised to try to come back for a visit with Teddy—without Fanny. But if Kitty had any say in it, Becky and Fanny would be joined at the hip from now on, especially since Becky had snuck out of her home this morning.

Once she was back in Teddy's car, Becky didn't feel like going home. The last thing she wanted to hear was a lecture on how bad her manners were. So, seeing that it was only a little before eleven, she decided to head off for downtown Savannah.

Part of her was ready to do a little shopping. But another part of her, the part that was really making the decision, wanted to see the apothecary Madame Cecelia had recommended. Perhaps there would be time to see Madame Cecelia too.

CHAPTER ELEVEN

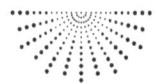

*S*avannah was bustling. Becky always felt a thrill of excitement when she made it into town. Ladies hurried along, carrying their parcels. Handsome gents tipped their hats to her as she drove by in Teddy's car.

The address of the apothecary Madame Cecelia had given was on the fringe of the bustling downtown area. It wasn't what most people considered a good neighborhood, but Becky had been to worse just to go dancing and have a drink. She pulled the car up in front of the display window and squinted to see inside. An awful glare on the window prevented her from seeing anything. After a yank of the parking brake, she shut off the car, climbed out, and approached the front door. It looked as if no one had entered through the front door in years. But the window advertised a cheery Open sign.

Before swallowing hard, Becky looked around. No one was paying any attention to her. And much to her surprise, no one was talking about Martha's birthday party. A shiver ran up her spine as she took hold of the handle, pulled the lever down with her thumb, and gave the door a push.

An angelic tinkling of bells sounded her arrival as she stepped into the store. It was dimly lit and smelled strongly of candles and incense that reminded Becky of church. As she walked down the main aisle, on each side of her stood a glass display case that stretched throughout the length of the store. Inside the display cases were exotic boxes of candy, scarves in bright colors, and tiny dishes with bizarre designs painted on them. There were beautiful pieces of jewelry like what Madame Cecelia had been wearing and delicate lace gloves, fans, and kerchiefs. But then Becky's eye was caught by a series of small pocket-sized books with titles like *Communications with the Dead* and *The Tarot*.

"Can I help you?"

The scratchy voice made Becky jump. She snapped her head in the direction the voice came from. Sitting there behind the counter was an old woman wearing a black dress with a black shawl and a black mantilla draped over her head. One of her eyes was white with cataracts.

"Oh, uh, I'm just looking. Thank you," Becky said politely. She felt herself staring at the blind eye and quickly looked down, pretending to study the sharp, daggerlike envelope openers in the case. One had a lovely silver handle in the shape of a peacock.

Feeling the old woman's one good eye on her, Becky proceeded to quickly admire the remaining things in the display case, working her way back toward the door. But before she could reach the door, the woman spoke again.

"You have to come back."

"What?" Becky snapped, feeling nervous.

"You have to come back." The old woman practically floated in Becky's direction. She didn't hear her footsteps or see the folds of her black dress move with her strides. "The spirits like you."

"I don't know what you're talking about." Becky tried to smile. That white eye bored into her.

"Of course you do... Rebecca."

"How do you know my name?" Just as Becky was about to dash out of the store, the little bells tinkled again. She whirled her head around, prepared to see a monster, a demon, a specter, but let out a loud gasp when she recognized Madame Cecelia.

"Mother, are you scaring the poor girl?"

Becky turned to see the old woman's face change from a threatening witch with ill intentions to a mischievous grandma type.

"What's going on?" Becky huffed. "I don't like people playing tricks on me."

"Believe me, Becky, had I known my mother was going to act this way, I would have met you down here myself. Mother, you owe Miss Becky an apology."

The old woman cackled with glee, waved her hand at Becky as if she couldn't be bothered, and went back to her perch where she'd been sitting when Becky first arrived.

"Don't mind her." Madame Cecelia shook her head. "My only worry about my mother is that when she dies, she's going to come back as a poltergeist and torment me even more than she does now."

"What's a poltergeist?" Becky asked.

"We'll have plenty of time to discuss that. Would you like some coffee?" Becky remembered the deep, rich smell of Lucretia's coffee, and it dawned on her she hadn't had a drop.

"I would. Thank you," Becky said while squinting

at Madame Cecelia, then she looked over her shoulder to her mother. "Is she coming?"

"You're very funny, Rebecca Madeline Mackenzie. Follow me." Madame Cecelia pulled the door to the drug store open and stepped outside. Becky followed her just a couple of steps to a heavy door with the numbers 784 ½ above it. There was something about addresses that included ½ that Becky always found intriguing. It was like they were mysteriously slipped in somehow.

"How do you know my whole name? Did Martha tell you?" Becky was still skeptical.

"No. Mr. Wilcox did," Madame Cecelia replied as she opened the other door and stepped inside, pointing Becky to a flight of stairs. "It's the first door on the left. Go on in."

Carefully and with her hand firmly on the banister, Becky went up the stairs. This place also smelled of incense and candles. When she reached the door, she took hold of the doorknob, and a shiver ran over her body from head to toe. Suddenly she felt light-headed and was afraid she was going to faint and fall backward down the stairs.

"Becky? Are you all right?" She heard Madame Cecelia's voice, but it was muffled, like Becky had cotton stuffed in her ears. When Becky turned, the entire hallway tilted, and she held onto the door-knob as if she might be tipped over if she didn't.

"My goodness. This is not what I expected at all. Mother!" Madame Cecelia shouted before rushing up to Becky and slipping her arm around her waist. Within seconds Becky saw the black form of Madame Cecelia's mother at the bottom of the stairs. As quick as a whip, she was at her side, her face contorted with worry, her blind eye softer than it had been. And it was the last thing she saw before everything went black.

When her eyes popped open, the first thing Becky saw was a rainbow of light from the most elegant Tiffany lamp she'd ever seen.

"She's got a severe case of the heebie-jeebies," she heard Madame Cecelia say. "I don't know if it was a good idea having her come here. Maybe I should have gone to her house."

"Too late now," the old woman muttered.

"What happened?" Becky sat up quickly, almost making her head swim again.

"Just relax," Madame Cecelia's mother said as she shuffled over to Becky's side. "We have a large family. We didn't expect them to rush you like they did."

"I feel like I'm burning with the blue flame, but

I haven't had a nip since yesterday at Martha's party." She looked around the room and only saw Madame Cecelia, who was sitting at a small card table by the window shuffling a deck of cards, and her mother, who was offering Becky a cup of strong black coffee. "Anything in this I should know about?"

"No," the old woman replied.

"Yeah, well, you just said you had a large family crammed in here. I don't know what kind of racket you two are running, but I'm thinking that maybe the guys in the white coats ought to visit the both of you." Becky swung her feet off the long sofa she was stretched out on and sat up straight, shaking the dizziness from her head.

"That's who greeted you at the door," Madame Cecelia said as she looked down at her cards. "They can be rather pushy when strangers come by, especially the ones who have been dead for a short amount of time. They have the most to say for some reason."

Becky took a sip of the hot coffee and peeked over the lip of the cup, watching Madame Cecelia and her mother's moves. The hot, bitter liquid was delicious and distracted her from what Madame Cecelia had just said. As soon as the words sank in, the coffee went down the wrong pipe, and she coughed.

"What?" Becky set the cup down on the end table and cleared her throat.

"Don't act surprised," the old woman scoffed. "My daughter says you can see them. She and I both can. It's a curse!"

"It's not a curse, Mother." Madame Cecelia rolled her eyes.

"It *is* a curse!" The old woman had been sitting in a straight-backed chair next to the couch but pushed herself up and walked over to her daughter. "I didn't like talking to your Cousin Mimi when she was alive. Now, she plagues me like a swarm of locusts from the grave."

"My mother has a flair for the dramatic," Madame Cecelia said, making her mother harrumph and leave the room, muttering to herself.

"Look, I appreciate the coffee," Becky said. "But I really don't know what you are talking about, and I think Martha has probably embellished any rumors or stories about me that she might have heard. She also has a flair for the dramatic."

"Martha never said anything to me. I can see it on you. It's like a pattern or maybe more like a birthmark." Madame Cecelia smiled. She was beautiful in the same way Becky's bedroom wallpaper was beautiful. She was different, unusual, and maybe just the right amount of tacky. But when Becky looked into Madame Cecelia's clear green eyes, she felt the woman could see more than Becky wanted her to.

"What do you want with me?" Becky snapped.

"I don't want anything. I'm making myself available to you because I see a storm coming." She looked back down at the table of cards.

"Don't you think you might be confusing me with Martha? After all, it was her house where there was a murder. I was in the dining room." Becky picked up the hot cup of coffee and took another sip. "And I barely knew the man."

"Ha-ha!" Madame Cecelia shook her head. Her smile pushed her cheeks up, revealing two deep dimples. "That doesn't matter to the spirits at work. Do you think it was a coincidence that that Ouija board made its first appearance and suddenly there was a death? A rather violent death, I might add."

Becky looked at Madame Cecelia and pointed her finger. "Are you saying it's Fanny's fault? Because good luck getting anyone in the Mackenzie family to admit she can do anything other than walk on water."

"Fanny is part of the puzzle, just like I am, just

like you are. Becky, I know that you have special talents. You don't have to worry about me thinking you are crazy or scary." Madame Cecelia tapped the rows of cards in front of her. "Quite the opposite. Frankly, I am jealous of your ability. It glows like the light magnified by those shards of crystal up there." She pointed to the chandelier overhead. "But if I can see it, so can the *Others*. You see what happened when you came to my front door, and those were just my family. The *Others* see you, too, except they are peeking from dark corners and around blind spots. I just want you to be careful."

Becky swallowed hard. She wasn't sure whether she believed all of this or if Madame Cecelia and her creepy mother were just playing a trick on her. Maybe they were afraid Becky was going to start doing parlor tricks too. Another psychic in town would impact their business. Not that Becky was a psychic. She wasn't. All she knew for sure about the future was that she would be having a drink and she would be doing some dancing.

"I'm going to go." Becky set the cup down and stood up. There was no dizzying residue. She felt fine and smoothed out the front of her dress. Then she noticed her stockings, with the tears and snags from scaling the trellis.

"You might want to stop in the store before you leave. Mother has something for you." Madame Cecelia smirked.

"What is it? A little tongue of newt? Maybe a charm to ward off the evil eye. She should know all about that," Becky said as she walked toward the door.

"Something you'll need." Madame Cecelia chuckled.

Becky stood at the door with her hand on the knob. For a moment she hesitated. What did Madame Cecelia know about her, and how did she come to know it? It had to be Martha or maybe Teddy. Perhaps at the party they let her secret slip. Teddy was three sheets to the wind. He wouldn't remember if he admitted to the murder of Lawrence Hoolihan, let alone Becky's secret life of conversing with the dead. Part of her wanted to stay with Madame Cecelia and talk. But she turned the knob, pulled the door open, and hurried down the stairs.

Without allowing herself time to think, she pushed the door to the apothecary open and stomped in a couple of steps before the white-eyed old woman stopped her. She held out a flat paper bag.

"You tell Adam White we said hello." The old woman chuckled.

Becky snatched the bag from the old woman and stomped out of the store, vowing never to return. She got in Teddy's car and opened the bag to find a brand-new pair of silk stockings.

"What did she mean by that? Tell Adam they said hello? How do they know Adam?" she muttered as she kicked off her shoes and pulled off her old, torn stockings. Within seconds, she wore her new ones and had left Teddy's car parked on the street while she continued stomping away from the apothecary. All Becky had had to eat was a sliver of Lucretia's corn bread and two deep sips of Madame Cecelia's delicious coffee. The tiny amount of food had left her feeling famished.

It only took a few minutes for her to spot the sign she was looking for. On the next block, straight ahead, was the word EAT. Her stomach grumbled at the idea, and as she walked in that direction with her head high, her red hair bouncing with each step, and her mind focused on what she'd just been through at Madame Cecelia's, she barely noticed the man who came out of the small door, carrying a stack of papers upon his strong shoulder. When she bumped into him and knocked the papers from his shoulder, she gasped.

"I'm so sorry," she said, the familiar smell of ink filling her nostrils.

"It's all right, Becky. Funny thing. I was just thinking about you," Adam White said with the same smile a little boy would have upon being presented with a surprise slice of apple pie.

CHAPTER TWELVE

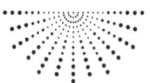

"What are you doing in the city all by yourself?" Adam asked as Becky nervously fidgeted with the cuffs of her dress.

"Oh. Well, I… uh… needed a new pair of stockings." It was the first thing that popped into her mind. She couldn't tell him she was visiting a fortune-teller and her crazy, white-eyed mother. "And I left the house so early that I didn't have any breakfast. So, I was going to get something to eat."

"Is that so?" he asked, that heavy northern accent of his making it sound like *"iz zat so."* "I hope you weren't thinking of going to this place." He jerked his thumb toward the diner with the EAT sign.

"I was."

"No. I won't let you. Come with me. I just have to

drop these bundles on the truck, and then I'll take you for breakfast." Adam once again stood dangerously close to Becky, looking down at her. "My uncle let me drive his car today. It's around back."

Before Becky could think twice, she felt herself nodding and the word "yes" tumbling out of her mouth. With a nod of his own, Adam smiled, picked up the bundles of newspaper, and hoisted them easily back onto his shoulders. They walked around the side of the building together to where the newspaper truck waited. He plunked the stacks on the truck bed and shouted to the driver. There was a honk just before the truck pulled away and disappeared down the other end of the alley.

"Come on." Adam took Becky by the hand and hurried back down the alley to the sidewalk, where an old jalopy was parked.

"This is your uncle's car?" Becky asked happily, sliding into the passenger seat after Adam held the door open for her.

"Sure is."

"He won't mind you driving me around?" Becky asked.

"Nope. I'm his favorite nephew," he replied as he got behind the wheel.

"And why is that?"

"Because I know all the pretty girls." He winked at Becky then made her squeal as he started the car and sped down the street.

Adam's uncle's car was an open top just like Teddy's. It was a little smaller and created a bigger cloud of gray smoke behind it, but as far as Becky was concerned, it was a chariot and she was a princess. Even when they rolled past the hen coop and half the ladies looking out the windows as they sat under the dryers recognized her, Becky didn't care. It was just the scandal needed to take the heat off Martha and the dead man they removed from her party. After all, Lawrence Hoolihan wasn't going to get any deader. But Rebecca Mackenzie cavorting around town with that Yankee Adam White was front-page news.

At first it was easy not to care. The sun was out, and the temperature was climbing. The smell of the jalopy's exhaust along with the sputter of its engine made Becky feel like she was a million miles from home. It was like she and Adam were the only two people in the world. They were no longer in the heart of Savannah but instead on the fringe of the city, where the buildings weren't so tall and time had braked to that wonderfully slow Southern speed.

"So where are you taking me?" Becky asked.

Without saying a word, Adam pointed at a small shack with peeling red paint and a wooden sign that read Good Food Here painted on it. Three other cars as well as a bicycle stood in front of the building. The front window had Phil's Diner painted across it in red-and-yellow letters along with mentions of stewed rhubarb and daily specials.

There were flower boxes loaded with wildflowers and patches of milk thistle growing up through the gravel drive.

When she saw the clock behind the dessert display inside the small joint, which smelled of strong coffee and sizzling bacon, she hiccupped. She hadn't realized how much time had passed since she left Rockdale Estate with Teddy's car. But then she looked at Adam, who had taken her hand and tugged her toward two empty seats at the counter.

As soon as they took a seat, Adam ordered two cups of coffee and a slice of apple pie for himself. Becky, who never met a cut of pig she didn't like, ordered herself bacon and a bowl of grits.

"So, I hear there was a bit of excitement at a party out in Pooler," Adam said, making Becky almost choke on her coffee.

"How did you hear about that?" Becky felt awful

that Adam knew about the party that he wasn't invited to.

"A murder is real news," he said.

Becky pinched her lips together and looked into Adam's blue eyes. "I thought for sure Martha would have come down with the screaming meemies, but she's doing all right. It was Lawrence Hoolihan. I didn't know him all that well, but…"

Adam gasped. "Larry? I had no idea that's who it was."

"You knew him?" Becky put her hand to her throat. "I'm so sorry."

"I can't say I'm surprised." Adam took a sip of coffee.

"Why?"

"He owed half of Savannah. The guy was a real louse. I don't think there was a card table in town that he didn't sit down at and lose. Big."

"It's funny you should say that. He was playing poker at the party." Becky had all but forgotten about the card she'd found on the floor. That card was snuggled against her breast as they spoke.

"You find out who was at that card table with him, and I'll bet dollars to donuts that you'll find who bumped him off," Adam said, his northern accent making him sound exotic and forbidden.

Becky, although she felt bad for poor Lawrence Hoolihan, couldn't really concentrate on *his* current state. He was dead. Murdered in cold blood. But right now, Becky was sitting so close to the sheik of her dreams, a real Valentino, that she would have been happy to talk about gutting a pig if it kept Adam White interested.

Finally, after finishing her grits and watching Adam devour two slices of pie in four bites, she looked again at the clock. It was already nearly one o'clock.

"Oh no." Her eyes bugged. "Is that really the time?"

Adam nodded.

"I'm so sorry, but you've got to take me back. I've got to get Teddy's car back to him. He's going to have kittens if I don't get back right away." She wiped her mouth and hopped off the stool as Adam tossed some change on the counter.

Before Becky even had a chance to thank him, they were in the car, heading back to the corner where they'd initially run into one another.

"Where did you park?" Adam asked as they neared the corner.

"You can drop me right here," Becky said. "I'm just around the corner. I think it's a one-way street," she lied, not wanting to risk running into Madame Cecelia or the old lady.

Without another word, Adam pulled the car to the curb and hopped out of his side to hurry and open the door for her.

"When will I see you again?" he asked, thrusting his hands deep in his pockets and leaning down an inch or two as if he couldn't hear Becky if he didn't. She could smell the ink on his clothes and wanted to drown in it.

"I'm sure I'll see you around," she gushed.

"Becky, I've been wanting to ask you something." He cleared his throat. "I hear it's a custom in these parts for a fellow to call on a lady when he wants to take her out on a proper date. Do you think… that is, would you mind if I came calling on you? Sometime?"

"I can't think of anything I'd like more," she stuttered.

"That's swell," he replied with a sly smirk. "Until then, will this be cash or check?"

"Why, Adam White. What are you trying to do? Ruin my reputation?" She giggled. Becky wanted nothing more than to throw her arms around his big, thick neck and kiss him full on the lips. But it was bad enough her mother was probably already aware she was in the Yankee's car. If anyone saw her necking in public, her mother would die of embarrassment. "This will have to be check. Thank you for breakfast."

Becky extended her hand as a proper lady would. Adam took it and squeezed it hard, making her knees quiver slightly. Once he let go, she sashayed down the street toward the apothecary and Teddy's car. She climbed in behind the wheel, started the engine, and within seconds began heading back home and to Rockdale Estate. She expected Teddy to be furious, but he wasn't even home.

She left the key with Mr. Rockdale, who had happily gotten his tractor to purr like the others. The problem was the belt, just as he'd said. But as Becky emerged from the path that joined the two pieces of property, she heard the cackle of a creature worse than whatever had swooped over her at Madame Cecelia's place. It was Fanny, and she was on the back porch with Teddy.

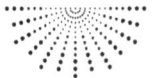

CHAPTER THIRTEEN

"*G*irl!" Teddy shouted. "Where in the world have you been?"

"I'm so sorry, Teddy. I lost track of time while I was running my errands." She had grabbed the tea towel Lucretia had given her this morning, which she'd hung on a bush along the way home. "I left the keys with your daddy. I returned her in one piece. Not a scratch." Becky winked.

"Rebecca, who is Adam White?" Fanny asked, her eyes narrowing like a cat spotting an unsuspecting mouse off in the distance.

"Adam White? I've heard the name but can't place the face. Works at the newspaper, I think. I can't be sure," she lied again.

"Your mother is fit to be tied over you and some

fellow named Adam White," Fanny said proudly. "If you don't know him, someone might be feeding your poor mother a line. I'd go talk to her if I were you."

Becky felt her chest tighten. It was bad enough Fanny was staying at the house, but to have her relaying messages to Becky on when to talk with her own mother, well, that was just too much. Without saying a word, Becky turned to the house and walked inside.

"Hi, Miss Becky," Lucretia said cheerfully.

"Hi, Lulu. Here's your towel back," Becky said, absently handing it back to the housekeeper. "Is my mother in the parlor?"

"She is," Lucretia replied.

After taking a deep breath, Becky marched down the hallway to the parlor, where her mother sat with her latest sewing project in her hands. She didn't look up when Becky entered the room.

"Hello, Ma—"

"I guess you didn't want Martha to be the only one with a scandal chasing behind her. Is that right?" Kitty asked.

"I am sure I don't know what you mean," Becky lied for the third time. She hated how easily lying came to her.

Kitty looked up at her daughter, her lips pinched together so hard they disappeared, leaving nothing but an angry slit in her face. "Rebecca Madeline, I received a visit from a very concerned Helen-Lyn Merryweather, who was at the beauty parlor getting her hair done when she saw my only daughter in the jalopy of a Mr. Adam White, who hails from enemy territory."

"Mama, please let me explain…"

"Now I am sure that the younger generation sees nothing wrong with welcoming the kin of those who beat, starved, and killed our family members in the great war of aggression, but I will not stand for it," Kitty said, looking back at her sewing.

"Mama, Adam White is as much a gentleman as any of the men born and raised here. Maybe even more so." Becky straightened her back. "In fact, like a real gentleman, he asked me if he could come calling on me some day, and I—"

"I hope you told him no!" Kitty finally looked her daughter in the eyes. "A real gentleman, indeed. He had no regard for what people were going to say about the two of you cavorting around town. Now all of a sudden he is going to act like a gentleman?"

"I told him I would like it very much if he did call

on me," Becky replied defiantly. "You'd like him, too, if you weren't so stuck in your ways."

"It's *these ways* that led me to marry so well. Had I been a recluse and fell for any man who paid me the slightest attention, I shudder to think of how my life could have turned out. Young lady, I just don't know where I've gone wrong." Kitty sighed. "Why can't you be more like your cousin Fanny?"

Becky felt like she'd been punched in the stomach. "Is that really what you want, Mama? You don't like me the way I am? Well, if you'll excuse me, I'm going to retire to my room for a spell. I've had an exhausting day and would like to wash my face before supper. If I may be excused."

Kitty's face made it obvious that she regretted what she'd said, but it didn't matter. The words were uttered aloud and could not be taken back. Without waiting for a reply, Becky left the parlor and nearly collided with Fanny, who had been studying a painting or a potted plant or the carpet or something that was close enough for her to hear every word.

It took every bit of energy for Becky to keep her tongue behind her teeth. Fanny's cheeks reddened as she tried to act casual, but she had clearly heard what Kitty had said and was relishing it.

Quietly and calmly, Becky went upstairs. Her

eyes started to sting with tears, but before they could breach her eyelids, she quickly shut her bedroom door and turned the lock.

How could her mother have said that to her when she knew how much Becky disliked Fanny? And she wasn't even willing to give Adam a chance just because he was a Yankee. If only Kitty knew how some of those Southern gentlemen acted at the juke joints and the speakeasies, she wouldn't be so quick to judge someone with a northern accent.

She sat down at her vanity and began to get undressed. The stockings Madame Cecelia's mother had given her held up nicely but not so nicely that she was willing to go back and visit. As she peeled off her dress and slip, the card with the devil face on it fell to the floor. Becky picked it up and studied it. If what Adam had said about Lawrence was correct, there was a good chance the murderer was at that small card table.

She was sitting there looking at the card when something tapped on her window. When she emerged outside and looked over the balcony railing, she saw Teddy.

"Fanny gave me the lowdown." He attempted to keep his voice at a raspy shout. "I'll pick you up at nine?"

"That sounds ducky. You are the bee's knees, Teddy. See you at nine." Becky waved before Teddy skipped off toward the well-worn path she had just come down minutes before.

Her problem now would be finding out who sat down at that poker table while Lawrence Hoolihan was there. That shouldn't be hard. There was only Coxy's Army at Martha's party.

Supper was quiet except for Fanny, who had a tale from Paris for every bite of food, every slight movement by Moxley, for everything. It was nerve-wracking. But Becky managed to swallow several mouthfuls.

"I am assuming you will be going out this evening." Kitty looked at Becky. "I fixed the zipper in your black dress if you wanted to wear it."

It was an olive branch, but Becky wasn't interested. Not yet. She loved her mother, and it hurt her heart not just emotionally but physically to be in a fight with her. She wouldn't have cared whether her mother approved of Adam or not. Time would win her over, and Becky knew that. But the comparison to Fanny was just one step too far. Becky might have overlooked that, had Fanny not been creeping just on the other side of the threshold like a spider. She heard Kitty. Becky didn't feel she deserved that humiliation, so she was going to stew.

"Thank you. May I be excused?" Becky could have eaten a few more bites of Lucretia's fried okra, but her desire to be alone was too strong.

"You barely ate anything," Judge said as he looked at his daughter. He had no idea what had transpired this afternoon, but as his eyes flitted from Becky to Kitty and back again to Becky, he was obviously figuring it out.

"I'm fine, Daddy. Just a slight headache is all." Becky stood from her chair. "I might soak in the tub for a spell."

"Would you like me to set your dress out for you?" Kitty asked.

"When I was in Paris, Granny Louise had a servant set my dresses out for that evening's events. The poor thing had absolutely no sense of style. I literally had to sit her down and tell her that pearls were for after eight," Fanny tittered, apparently oblivious that no one was listening to her. "Why, I had to just pull the clothes out of the closet for myself if I wanted to be out of the house on time. The poor thing wasn't from Paris. I believe Granny Louise said she was from... oh, I don't know. One of those countries where they don't pay much attention to how they look."

"No. I can tend to myself," Becky said plainly before leaving the room. She could have pulled the same stunt as Fanny and lingered just out of view from the dining room and listened to what was said. But regardless of her mother's wish, Becky was determined to never be like Fanny. That girl might have had the wool pulled over everyone else's eyes, but Becky was wise to her.

Lucretia and Moxley had been with the Mackenzie family as far back as Becky's first memory. But throughout the years they had had a slow turn of different housekeepers. Beatrice had been with them the longest, for almost twenty years, but was then consumed by pneumonia after an unnatural cold had gripped the South a decade ago. Then, after much searching, they found Theresa Mae. Becky liked her a lot. She was a pretty woman with the smoothest black skin Becky had ever seen. As a little girl she'd often ask to touch her cheek, and Theresa would laugh and oblige her. She was a good maid. But she was married, and her husband was a fine man who had dreams of moving to Chicago to start his own business. After working for the Mackenzies for almost seven years, Theresa announced she was quitting and leaving for the Midwest. Of course, the family wished her luck and set about finding her replacement. That was when they found Dolores.

"Did I hear you saying you'd be wanting to take a bath, Miss Becky?" Dolores rarely spoke above a whisper. She was full figured, and anyone who saw her coming might expect a big, booming voice with an attitude to match. But there was no gentler soul than Dolores.

"I did, Dolores. Would you mind running the bath water for me?"

"Of course not. Let me put these here linens up, and I'll be right with you." Her voice was so high that she sounded like a little girl. She was not married and lived in a tiny room no bigger than a closet just off the kitchen.

As gentle as a lamb but as reliable as an ox, Dolores had become a valued employee of the Mackenzie family and a trusted confidant to Becky.

With the tub almost full of hot water, she added a few drops of lavender oil and put out three thick heavy towels.

"I know your mama doesn't like for more than one towel to be used per bath, but I won't tell if you won't," Dolores said more than once to Becky, who she knew loved to wrap one towel around her body and one around her shoulders and use the last to dry her feet.

"You're a good egg, Dolores. I have some chocolate in my room in the third drawer of my nightstand. Why don't you help yourself to a couple of pieces," Becky said as she proceeded to remove her jewelry.

"Miss Becky, can I tell you something?"

"Of course, Dolores." Becky turned from the tub and looked at the maid.

"I heard what your mama said this afternoon." She swallowed hard. "You know she didn't mean that. I've heard her with the ladies from the Christian Ladies League, and she brags on you something fierce."

Becky felt tears stinging her eyes.

"She's not like you. What people think means something to her. She ain't broke of those chains like you are. Don't begrudge her that." Dolores smiled. "She only fuss over Fanny because she like a new doll. She'll be tired of her soon enough. But Miss Kitty ain't never goin' to tire of you."

"What would I do without you, Dolores?" Becky said as she walked across the bathroom and kissed the woman's plump cheek.

"You'd be dryin' with just one pitiful towel." Dolores giggled as she backed out of the bathroom and shut the door.

Becky undressed and slipped into the hot, fragrant water. With a deep sigh, she let her body relax. In just a few hours she would climb out her window again and meet Teddy to head out to anywhere but here. This time, she'd take her stockings with her and put them on in the car instead of risking their getting shredded on the way down the trellis again.

Mama's going to want you to take Fanny. The thought interrupted her plan like a slap across the face. Well, if it had to be that way, fine. Becky could take the high road if she had to. She didn't like it, but she'd do it.

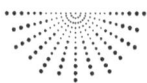

CHAPTER FOURTEEN

"*I* don't see why you had to climb down the side of the building," Fanny huffed as Becky climbed into the rumble seat of Teddy's car and proceeded to put on her silk stockings.

"I didn't want to run into Mama." Becky thought the tone of her voice was enough to indicate she didn't want to continue this topic of conversation. But like with everything, Fanny had to present her two cents' worth.

"Rebecca, I think you are being too hard on your dear mama."

"Do you?" Becky snapped as she carefully rolled one stocking and slipped it over her toes.

"She's not completely wrong. If people see you gamboling with the wrong kind of man, you aren't just ruining your reputation but theirs too." Fanny batted her long false eyelashes.

"If I were gamboling with the wrong kind of man, I could agree with you. But Adam White is not the wrong kind of man. Mama is wrong. She's *my* mother. I should know," Becky replied without looking up from snapping her garter to her stocking.

Teddy let out a whistle that made Becky roll her eyes and shake her head. She was glad he did it and cut the tension from the car ride.

"You better keep your eyes on the road. Where are we headed?" Becky asked as she adjusted the skirt of the black dress her mother had fixed the zipper on.

"How about Willie's?" Teddy looked back at Becky.

"You were reading my mind!" She clapped.

"What's Willie's?" Fanny asked innocently. As Teddy told her about the place and its huge dance floor, great music, and strong drinks, Becky couldn't help but think that back in Paris, Fanny probably gave quite a few gents an education. This babe-in-the-woods act wasn't fooling her.

"That sounds just ducky. You will stick close to me, I hope." Becky watched Fanny put her hand on Teddy's shoulder.

"The whole gang will be there. You'll fit right in," he chirped.

"Everyone but Lawrence Hoolihan," Becky said. "Teddy, do you happen to know who he was playing poker with last night?"

"I haven't a clue. Why?"

"Well, I was just theorizing that maybe he'd gotten into a bit of trouble with another gent at the poker table and it ended badly. You know Martha didn't know everyone who showed up." Becky smoothed her hair out of her face. "Some of them were friends of friends of friends and obviously not the kind of people who took their poker lightly."

"I think it was those Gypsies," Fanny said, lifting her chin. "It was obvious they were shady characters. I don't know what would make Martha think it was a good idea to allow them in the house."

"They stood out like sore thumbs. It wasn't them," Becky said as she recalled how she was treated at Madame Cecelia's apartment.

"Of course it was. People like that drift through towns stealing all the time," Fanny insisted. "If this Lawrence fellow was playing poker, I'll bet that Count Ernesto saw he was winning and decided to get him alone. Lawrence probably put up a fight, leaving the man with no choice but to kill him. They are dirty people."

"I'm telling you it wasn't them." Becky felt herself getting flustered with Fanny. She wanted to tell the woman to just shut up about things she didn't know but instead tried to be reasonable. She knew she was coming across like a spoiled brat, just what Fanny would enjoy. "That Count Ernesto was entertaining quite a few of the ladies. They were fawning all over him. I think the last thing on his mind was a poker game. And I was with Madame Cecelia just before you started screaming."

"Becky, I know Martha is your friend. You can't bring yourself to attribute any blame for what happened on her." Fanny looked down her nose as she turned to Becky. "But trust me, I know. My world is much bigger than Savannah. I know things about people that you would just have no way of knowing because you've lived such a sheltered life."

"Horsefeathers!" Becky snapped. Then she bit her tongue. There was no use ruining the evening. With a few more twists and turns, they'd be at Willie's, and she could have a nice strong drink and stay on the dance floor, as far away from Fanny as possible.

"Frankly, I don't think either one of you dames is correct. Out of all three of us, I knew Lawrence

Hoolihan the best, and I barely knew the guy," Teddy interrupted.

"So, Sherlock, what is your theory?" Becky asked, happy he had jumped into the conversation.

"I think he did it to himself." Teddy said with a confident smirk. Fanny gasped as if the concept had escaped her normally razor-sharp brain. Becky burst out laughing.

"I'm serious," Teddy whined. "He went to get some cake, slipped after having too much to drink, and fell on the knife."

"Teddy, you do know the man was stabbed in the back. Right square in the middle of his back," Becky said in between chuckles.

Fanny put one hand to her mouth and the other over her stomach.

"It could happen." Teddy defended his position. "You do remember when Mortimer Riley was kicked by that mule."

Becky began to laugh even harder. "What does that have to do with Lawrence Hoolihan getting stabbed?"

"That mule got him right square between the eyes. The horseshoe print was dead center on his forehead. You couldn't have placed it there intentionally if he were tied to a chair and ossified." Now

Teddy started to laugh. "Remember, he had a bruise in that shape on his face for weeks. And it didn't kill him. How's that for an example of the impossible being possible?"

By this time, Becky had begun wiping the corners of her eyes as she laughed even harder. Fanny sat stone-faced in the passenger seat. "I don't think this is the kind of topic people should be laughing at." She shifted in her seat.

Of course, that was all it took for Becky and Teddy to laugh even more.

"You two don't know how devastating, how horrifying it was to be the one to discover that man. He practically fell right on top of me," Fanny said with wide eyes. "I'm convinced it was the Gypsies. I know Martha's family, and they would never have anything to do with that kind of riffraff even if they were there to do parlor tricks. They probably live on skid row, and after this incident they probably packed up their belongings in bed sheets tied to a stick and headed off for the next town. That was all Martha's idea to have them. I can promise you that."

"I don't know. I saw that Ernesto guy pull a foot and a half of rope with a silver doodad at the end of it from Pete's ear," Teddy added. "If they were a couple of shucksters, they were talented."

The mention of Ernesto made Becky realize he was not at the apartment when she went to visit Madame Cecelia. For some reason, she assumed they resided together, but perhaps he had his own place.

"Well, they were nothing like the fortune-teller that I saw in Paris," Fanny insisted.

"What was the difference?" Becky asked, hating herself for having any interest in what Fanny Doshoffer had to say.

"Well, there is a world of difference between how things are done in France and how they are done here." Fanny lifted her chin again as she spoke. "It isn't necessarily better, but they just have that quality to them that elevates them. Every person we encountered thought I was from Paris. That's how easily I fit in."

Becky let Fanny ramble on. She obviously wouldn't answer her question. Even if she did, she'd probably say something that made Becky even more annoyed, so it was probably best that she let things go. For now.

Finally, they reached Willie's. Becky was happy to stretch her legs as she climbed out of the rumble seat and vowed to call shotgun on the way home. The parking lot was filled with cars.

"My, we'll be lucky to get a seat," Fanny said as

she slipped her arm through Teddy's and pulled closer to him.

"I don't plan on sitting for a second," Becky said as she hurried ahead. "Wait a minute! Is that Delilah and Zachary?"

Making as big a scene as possible, Becky stopped and pointed at a couple who had been enjoying a romantic moment alone in an adorable two-seat speedster.

"It is! You two devils! Come up for some air!" Becky teased.

"Hi, Becky!" Delilah said, waving.

"Perfect timing, Becky!" Zachary chuckled.

Having already forgotten about Fanny and her French philosophy, Becky hurried to the entrance, which consisted of a single door under a cool blue light down a few concrete steps from sidewalk level. Her skirt shimmied, and her red hair bounced with every step. She stood on her tiptoes as she knocked on the door. A small window opened, and a deep voice boomed from inside.

"Well, if it isn't my favorite redhead." The little window shut, and the door opened. It was like stepping into heaven. The smell of cigarettes filled Becky's nose. The music was loud, and whoever was on the drums beat that snare so hard she could feel it in her chest.

"Hiya, Hank. How's tricks?" Hank was the doorman at Willie's. If Hank said you weren't coming in, you weren't coming in. The tuxedo he wore made him look even bigger than the six feet four that he actually was. His shoulders were so wide that he had to go through almost every door sideways, and his mitts were the size of porterhouse steaks.

"No complaints. No one will listen."

"Teddy and some dame are bringing up the rear." Becky winked as she jerked her thumb over her shoulder. "There they are."

"Who's the tomato?" Hank asked. He was no different from any other man around. The only way a fellow wouldn't notice Fanny was if he were blind or dead. And even then, Becky had her doubts.

"Oh, that's Miss Trouble with capital T."

"I like that kind of trouble," Hank replied as he looked Fanny up and down.

"Well, some people like spinach," Becky said again, standing on her tiptoes to adjust Hank's bow tie before clapping him on the cheek.

"Teddy, keep an eye on her," Hank said, looking

down at Becky as Teddy and Fanny slipped through the door. "She's on a roll."

"Will do." Teddy saluted the big man and slipped past him with Fanny in tow.

As they made their way through the tables, Becky couldn't advance a foot without someone waving or calling her name. Pretty ladies in expensive dresses came and gave her a hug or offered her a sip of their drinks. Some fellows politely kissed her hand, while others who were more brazen kissed her cheek. She never swatted a single one away and smiled instead, nodding to the promise of a trip around the dance floor.

"I didn't realize so many people knew Becky," Fanny said with a hint of disappointment in her voice.

"Becky is the bee's knees. If you don't like Becky, there is something wrong with you," Teddy said casually as he scanned the faces in the crowd. "Aha! There they are!"

He frantically started to wave and pull Fanny through the crowd to where three tables of four were pushed together. Martha waved wildly as Teddy and Fanny approached.

"Don't tell me Becky didn't come." She frowned. "Oh, I knew I shouldn't have had her help clean up today."

"Becky helped you clean up?" Fanny asked.

"She's such a dear. Of course she came by to help. I don't think there has ever been a party at the Bourdeaux household where Becky didn't come back the following day to help clean up. Of course, a lot of the times, we'd clean up the remaining hooch, but today it was a sober event." Martha frowned again.

"No. She's here. She was just in front of us a second ago." Teddy slipped out of Fanny's grip and circled around to Martha. She looked up into his eyes, and he put his finger under her chin, raising it to him. "How are you holding up?"

"I'm doing just fine. Just need a little hair of the dog that bit me. But I swear I don't think I'll ever be able taste a piece of birthday cake again without vomiting," Martha joked as she pulled out a seat for Teddy next to her.

"Teddy, are you going to get us some drinks?" Fanny asked as the man on the other side of Martha stood and offered her his seat.

"Absolutely. I'm the Sahara Desert. What can I get you?" Teddy clicked his tongue and winked.

"I think I'd like one of those gin rockies," Fanny replied.

"You mean a gin rickey?" Teddy corrected her.

"Oh, yes. Of course." Fanny batted her eyelashes and smiled.

"And for you? Your regular?" Teddy asked Martha.

"You're reading my mind." She giggled. "So stop it! You'll read something you shouldn't have."

"I'll be back in a jiffy." Teddy sashayed through the crowd toward the bar.

"He'll be back in an hour," Martha joked. She had already had a few drinks and was feeling calm and content.

Just then, Becky and a gent named Norman nearly collided into the table, laughing and sweating.

"This band is swinging!" Becky said. "I was on my way over here to see you, and Norm just scooped me up. And you know I'm a sucker for a handsome face."

"How about it, Becky? Cash or check?" Norman asked, leaning closer for a kiss. He had hair as red as Becky's and a swarm of freckles across the bridge of his nose.

"Sorry, Norm. The bank is closed."

"I'll bet it won't be if Adam White shows up." Norm playfully nudged Becky in the ribs.

"Norman, I'm sure I don't know what you are talking about. Adam White and I are friends. Is there anything wrong with that?"

"He's a lucky duck," Norman replied. "I'm going to go iron my shoelaces. Dance with me later?"

"Just say when." Becky picked up a paper napkin and dabbed her forehead with it as Norm hustled away toward the men's room. "He's a good egg."

"He is. I am surprised he doesn't have a steady girl," Martha said just before she threw back the last gulp in her glass.

Suddenly, another man snuck up behind Becky and put his hands around her eyes before leaning close to her ear. "Guess who."

"Why, President Harding. How did you ever find me here?" Becky replied. When the young man removed his hands and Becky turned around, she squealed with surprise. "Sam Lustyk. You devil. I heard you had left for Charlotte, North Carolina."

"I did. But I heard you were going to be here and travelled all those miles just to ask you to take a spin around the dance floor." Sam was tall, as thin as a reed, and a great dancer.

"What are we waiting for?" Becky took a quick gulp from someone's glass on the table before letting Sam pull her close for a foxtrot.

Martha looked sideways at Fanny. She recorded the look on the woman's face so that when she talked to Becky alone she could recall every tiny detail. It would make Becky's day.

"She's a lot different when she's not at home," Martha said with a smile.

"I'll say." Fanny shifted in her seat. "I had no idea."

"She loves to dance, and she's really good at it. When she and I first started hitting the speakeasies, I was a shy, awkward mess. I worried if I had the steps right and how I looked. Becky didn't care one bit. She danced with anyone and got better and better every time. That's why the fellas chase her down." Martha picked up one glass then another. Then she clicked her tongue in disgust. "Look at all these dead soldiers. Where is Teddy?"

"Did I hear someone say my name?" Teddy carefully set down three tall drinks then took a seat next to Martha. Within just a few minutes, Becky came back, sweating and smiling until she realized something was missing.

She frowned. "Hey, where's my drink?"

Teddy rolled his eyes, stood up, and went back to the bar. Becky took his seat. "When are you going to get out there, Martha?" Becky asked.

"Oh, it's early, and I haven't had nearly enough to drink."

"What about you, Fanny?" Becky said. "I don't

have to tell you that there are a couple of gents sizing you up as we speak. Give them a wink and go take a twirl."

"Oh, I'm not feeling like it just yet. Besides, in Paris, things were done a little differently. A lady didn't just jump into things with both feet. I guess I'm just a little used to taking my time."

Becky shrugged then put her elbow on the table to hold her chin in her hand. "So, how are Mr. and Mrs. Bourdeaux doing now that all the excitement has died down?"

"Mother insists we need to have Father Bartholomew come bless the house again. She's also sorely disappointed in her twenty-one-year-old daughter who can go out dancing after such a traumatic event." Martha sipped her drink.

"You think you've got it bad? Kitty knows about Adam White," Becky grumbled.

"What? What happened? How? Did he come calling? Oh, tell me what he was wearing. I'll bet he looked dapper." Martha swooned.

"No. Nothing so proper. In fact, it was a downright indecent display, right, Fanny?" Becky looked over at the blonde, who sneered. "I was spotted in the front seat of Adam's jalopy driving down Main Street."

"So who ratted you out?" Martha turned to Fanny. "Good Lord, you didn't."

"I had nothing to do with it," Fanny replied with her chin raised.

"Helen-Lyn Merryweather. She spied me through the window of the beauty parlor. I wonder if she arrived with curlers in her hair or if she waited for the stylist to finish before she hightailed it to Mama's house."

Martha had to hold her hand over her mouth to prevent herself from spitting up her drink. "Oh, that would be a sight. Watching her with half her hair pinned while she waddled at full speed down the front walk." Martha laughed. "My goodness, the woman is as wide as she is tall."

"Now, Martha, I do hope you'll talk some sense into your friend here," Fanny interrupted. "Her mother has every right to be upset. I hear Adam White—that is his name, right? I hear he's a Yankee and he works at the newspaper. That's hardly the kind of career a man should have if he's serious about a woman."

"Fanny...?" Martha started.

"Aunt Kitty just wants the best for Rebecca," Fanny continued. "And being seen with a man of an ill reputation is not what's best. When I was in Paris, only the men of the highest caliber approached me. Granny Louise made sure of that."

Finally, Teddy returned with Becky's drink. She stood to give him back his seat. She'd had enough talk about Kitty and Adam and certainly didn't want to listen to anything else that Fanny might have had to say.

"Where are you going?" Teddy asked.

"My ice isn't cold enough." She shook her drink and headed off into the crowd at the bar. As much as she loved being at Willie's—and it was her favorite speakeasy—she was not herself this evening. She blamed her mother. Becky was sure that when she was born, the old girl put a hex on her so that any time Kitty did something to upset her, it would be *her* that felt the guilt. She strolled until she found an empty seat at the bar. She pulled a cigarette from her clutch and was searching for a match when a flame flickered right in front of her face. She took hold of the male hand, held the match to her cigarette, and looked up to see none other than the Heathcliff boy.

"Hey, Becky. Long time no see," he said with a silly grin on his face.

"Oh, hello. Fancy meeting you here," Becky replied, still unable to remember his first name.

"That was some excitement last night. Everyone

is talking about it," he said. "I wouldn't be surprised if Martha never showed her face again."

"Martha is right over there with Teddy and Fanny and heaven knows who else. Why don't you go say hello?" Becky said encouragingly, but the Heathcliff boy didn't pick up on it.

"That Fanny sure is pretty," he said, looking in the direction Becky had pointed. "You don't like her because she's always trying to upstage you."

"That's about right," Becky replied before taking a drink and then a puff on her cigarette.

"I don't think she holds a candle to you, Becky." The Heathcliff boy kept talking, but he didn't look away from where Fanny, Martha, and Teddy were sitting. "Having a girl like that would be nothing but trouble. She's the kind of girl that can't be trusted. She talks too much."

"That's for sure. If I hear the word Paris again, I think I'll upchuck." Becky laughed. But she was alone in her amusement. The Heathcliff boy looked at her. He didn't look like a guy out to have a good time. He looked like he'd just discovered he would have to take a test and anyone who failed it would be doomed to live in mud for the rest of their lives.

"You don't talk too much," he continued. "In fact, I bet you know how to be very discreet." Becky blinked as she watched the Heathcliff boy's face. Was he joking? Was he trying to be funny and completely missing the mark? He smiled down at her and gave her a playful tap on the arm. "Can I get you another drink?"

"Uh, no. I have to go powder my nose." She slipped off the stool and started to walk toward the ladies' room.

"I'll save your seat."

"You do that," Becky said as she made her way in the direction of the ladies' room. But suddenly, she had a terrible thought. What if the Heathcliff boy was waiting outside the ladies' room when she came out? She didn't want to talk to him anymore. He was giving her the heebie-jeebies.

Just then, Hank appeared. "Hey, doll. You lost?"

CHAPTER FIFTEEN

"*H*ank. Thank goodness. I'm trying to give this guy the slip. Can you help me out?" She folded her hands in front of her. "Pretty please?"

"Sure. Come with me." He took Becky's hand in his, and it completely disappeared within the folds of his palm. "Now you can look around, but these guys like it quiet, so just try and behave."

"I'll do my best." She squeezed his hand. They went around one corner and then another until they came to a set of swinging doors to a kitchen that was closed for the night.

The burners were cold. The pots and pans had been scrubbed and were hanging from hooks. Dishes, cups, and saucers were neatly stacked in towers. And in the middle of everything were two card tables with serious-looking men sitting there and piles of money in the middle of them all.

A few pretty girls milled around, chatting with one another quietly. Becky couldn't help but notice that some of them had some serious ice on their fingers or around their necks or dangling from their wrists.

"Everything okay back here, boys?" Hank asked.

The men nodded or grunted their replies. There was a guy behind a small bar just beyond the tables.

"She's with me. Red, say hello to the fellas."

Becky smiled, lifted her chin, and gave a wink and a wave. She knew a couple of these fellas were probably packing heat. They weren't the kind of characters she would care to run into in a dark alley. But here, they were much more interested in the cards in their hands than in her.

"Go get yourself a drink, doll. I'll be back in a few minutes," Hank said.

"Thanks," she replied and flounced over to the bar. After taking a seat and ordering herself a gin rickey from the bartender, who looked like he'd only just started wearing long pants, Becky turned to the game at the table closest to her.

"So, how come a pretty girl like you is hiding out here?" the bartender asked.

"I'm trying to lose a real flat tire," she said and took a sip of her drink. "How about giving me the skinny on what's going on here?"

"Sure. Well, you see..." The bartender started with his voice just above a whisper. He went on to tell Becky who was winning, who was losing, and how much was in the kitty. But he never mentioned any of their names, which was probably for the best. Becky studied their faces. She imagined Martha's parlor the prior night with the men at the poker table. She was sure that dealer was at Martha's.

"They're here every night?" Becky asked.

"Rooney!" one of the men shouted in their direction and waved his empty glass. The bartender nodded before giving Becky a wink and turning his back to mix the man another round. Then Becky saw another fellow come in. Actually, he just sort of appeared from the shadows.

He looked like one of the hobos she'd seen hopping off the boxcars in the middle of Savannah sometimes. His clothes were old and out of style, dirty and worn. His back was stooped, and wild whiskers grew on his face. His hair was a nest of gray, unkempt strands that stood on end. His hands were what captivated her. They had long, elegant fingers, like those of someone who might have played the piano or even the harp. At the ends of each finger were long nails, thick and yellow.

Becky continued to watch as he shuffled up to the table of card players. No one seemed to pay him any mind. It was as if they couldn't see him. Without hesitating, the bum took his place behind the man who was shuffling the deck. Everyone else in the room was going about as if the fellow wasn't even there. Then it hit Becky that maybe he was there but no one else could see him. As if the thought had caught his attention, the hobo looked up and grinned at Becky. He exposed two rows of yellow teeth that were jumbled up in his mouth. There were black spaces where some had rotted out. Still others were partially consumed by cavities yet clung to the gray gums.

As he stared, he pulled a cigar from the inside pocket of his coat, stuffed it in his mouth, and with one wooden matchstick dragged across his whiskered cheek, lit the cigar. With each puff, the smoke swirled around his head and fell in translucent layers over the table. Still, the men showed no indication that they noticed the guy.

With that sinister smile still on his face, the old

hobo leaned close to the dealer, whispering something to him. How could he be doing that? Those other men should be crying foul.

Suddenly, a shiver ran over her. The air grew cold, and the sound of the music from the main room that was thumping through the walls became even more muffled. As she watched the men talk and banter with one another, their voices sounded hushed, like she was listening to them from underneath a heavy blanket.

The experience reminded her of the time she had had one too many sips of moonshine that one of her neighbors had brought to a party down by the river.

"Hey, is it getting darker in here?" She tried to speak, but her voice came out like a squeak. She tried and tried to shout, but it was like she was screaming into water. Panic seized her, and she looked at the bum, who stared right at her as he continued to whisper in the dealer's ear. Then, as if that weren't bad enough, he extended his arm and pointed at her. One long bony finger extended, the thick yellow nail curving slightly at the end.

The dealer looked up and saw Becky staring at him.

Her heart pounded in her chest. She didn't know what she was afraid of, but she was terrified. Never in her life had she felt such icy-cold fingers slithering through her gut. She snapped her eyes away from the shabby old man and looked directly at the dealer. He blinked, looked down at his cards, and began the game.

Becky swallowed hard. Just as quickly as the silence had settled over the room, everything popped back to life again, making Becky lose her balance and fall off her stool.

"Good heavens!" One of the ladies who had been deep in conversation quickly rushed over. She had hair so blond it was almost white. "Are you all right? I thought you were starting to look a little green around the gills, honey."

"I don't know what happened," Becky said as she got to her feet. "I just lost my balance or something." She looked over at the poker table. One of the gents was standing, ready to come to her aid, but she waved him off. The hobo was nowhere to be seen.

"Rooney, give her a snort," the blonde said.

Becky took the shot, tossed it back, and then smoothed out her skirt. "Feel better?"

"I do. I think I better get back to my friends." She pointed at the swinging doors. Just then, she noticed the dealer staring at her. He looked as if he'd seen a ghost. Becky swallowed hard and carefully looked behind her to see if he really was looking at her. Part of her expected to see the grimy hobo standing behind her, but he wasn't there. When she looked back at the table, she saw the face of the yellow-eyed devil staring back at her. That face was on the deck of cards, just like the one she'd found at Martha's house. Suddenly, her energy came rushing back. She watched as the dealer took his cards and excused himself. One of the guys from the other table quickly took his place.

"Do you know that guy?" Becky asked the blonde.

"Nope. This is the first time I've seen him," she said, watching him leave.

"Hey, thanks a million for your help. I'm feeling much better," Becky said and took a few steps toward the swinging door.

"Don't mention it, honey." The blonde waved as if this were an everyday occurrence and nothing out of the ordinary. "Poor kid can't hold her liquor," Becky heard her say. Little did she know that Becky was more than capable of holding her liquor, but this was not a case of being lit. Something else was going on, and those devil cards were part of it.

As Becky followed the guy from the kitchen down the hallway and back to the dance hall, she tried to remember if he was at Martha's party. He wasn't a very striking man. He didn't dress particularly nicely, nor was his face easy to peg. He stopped at the coat check, and Becky watched him give the check girl a five-dollar bill. The girl giggled as he said a few things to her, and then out the door he went. Quickly, Becky made her move.

"Hiya," Becky said to the coat-check girl. "That big palooka who just slipped you a five. Do you know his name?"

"Sure. He goes by Diggs. You aren't his moll, are you?"

"Me? No!" The thought of dating a gangster was worse than trying to date a Yankee, although to Kitty it might be a step up. "I saw him at a party and wanted to say howdy-do. Thanks," Becky said and dropped a nickel in her tip jar.

When Becky approached the door, Hank gave her a serious look.

"Leaving so early? I hope the boys didn't give you a hard time." He looked concerned.

"Oh, you, stop. I'm just going out for some air. And no, the boys were complete gentlemen," Becky said as she stood on tiptoes and pinched Hank's cheek.

"Well, now I know you're lying. Those guys ain't

been called gentlemen since they were in short pants. And maybe not even then," he retorted.

"Not all of them can be like you, Hank. I'll be back in a jiffy," she said as she went outside.

People were milling around out there. The night air was refreshing and felt downright chilly compared to the club. Becky climbed the steps to the sidewalk and looked around. Standing perfectly still, she listened and heard footsteps clomping off to her right. It had to be Diggs.

Just beyond the parking lot were a lot of trees. They muffled the noise and cut down the view from the main streets, and even though the police knew what was going on every night at Willie's, they looked the other way most of the time. Half of them would show up for a nip after their shift. Becky was willing to bet on that. A slight breeze rustled the leaves and carried the smell of grass and moss on it. Becky squinted and saw Diggs head toward the line of trees.

Carefully, she followed. Just on the other side of the tree line was civilization again, consisting of a couple of rows of apartment buildings and a motel or two. It wasn't skid row, but it wasn't the kind of place Becky wanted to be caught alone. This part of town was nothing like downtown Savannah. It was a perfect place for a speakeasy but not a great place to be walking at this hour of the night.

Finally, Becky caught up to the footsteps and saw Diggs's silhouette. She dreaded the idea of following him into the woods. No one would know she'd gone in there. If anything happened, it would be months before they found her.

"Stop that, Becky," she muttered. "You're just looking around. No one would be out to kill you. That murder was over a cheat in a card game. That's all." Her words, even though they came from her mouth, were not very convincing. Still, she continued to creep along behind him.

Was there another joint around? A dump could pop up overnight like a toadstool and disappear just as quickly. Diggs walked a few more paces and then froze. Becky did the same thing. Had he heard her? Did he know he was being followed?

Then Becky saw Diggs pull something from his pocket and toss it on the ground. He took a few more steps and then stopped, whirling around and staring in her direction. Becky ducked behind an old Flivver and held her breath. He stood there for a few moments. He couldn't possibly see her, could he?

Like a deer that had picked up on a scent, Diggs bolted into the woods, leaving Becky standing alone at the edge of the parking lot. She had seen him toss away something and was determined to find out what.

Carefully she crept up to where she thought he might have stood. She looked along the ground. Anyone who saw her would have thought she was looking for her keys or that maybe her glasses had fallen off, if she wore glasses. The grass tickled her calves, and she was sure the soft dirt would ruin her shoes. But she didn't care. She had to see what Diggs had tossed away.

Just as she was about to give up and head back inside, Becky saw it. It was a deck of cards. As she reached down to pick up the box, she saw the same yellow-eyed devil. Then two gunshots rang out. Suddenly coated in a thick layer of sweat, Becky ducked down in the grass and held her breath.

Someone was running. Someone a lot lighter on their feet than Diggs would have been. Finally, emerging from the line of trees was a short, thin fellow. He was dressed in a suit and fedora, but other than that, he was just a black form. He walked like a man on his way home from work. Becky didn't move. The only thing worse than being the target of a hit was being some unlucky schlub who witnessed it and gave away their hiding place. If she moved, if she sneezed, if she did anything, that black form would turn on his heel and saunter just as casually in her direction and find her.

Finally, the man disappeared around the back of the club. She heard a car start. When the headlights cut through the shadows as the vehicle swung around the building, Becky ducked down farther into the tall grass. The car rolled away slowly. The driver was in no hurry.

Until Becky was sure she no longer heard the car, she waited. The muffled sound of the music from the club and a few random crickets were all she could hear now. Her heartbeat had steadied and was no longer pounding in her ears. And the breath she'd been holding came out with a long sigh.

Without thinking, she stood up, relieving her thighs, which had been burning from her crouched position, and smoothed out her skirt. The desire to go and see if Diggs was dead overpowered her. She took two steps in the direction the dark form had come from but stopped. Were there footsteps behind her? She squinted into the darkness. Nothing.

Carefully, she took another couple of steps while holding onto the thin trees all around her for balance. But an overwhelming sensation that she was walking into a trap made her stop. She was squeezing one thin tree trunk with one hand and the deck of cards with the other.

"Hey, Becky!" a voice hissed from in front of her. "Need a light?"

Becky strained to see. In the flash it took for a match to light, Becky saw the old hobo's face. He grinned. As the little flame flickered, he looked even more weather worn. In the orange glow, she saw the slit of his mouth reveal uneven teeth and black holes where teeth should have been. A tongue slithered out, licked his lips, and retreated into his maw before he started laughing.

Without realizing it, Becky screamed. And she screamed loudly. Her instincts kicked in, and she darted in the direction of the club. Her heels sank into the ground, and her skirt snagged on a couple of bushes, but still she ran. The sound of the old bum's laughter was getting louder. She was sure he was getting closer to her. Just as she was about to break the tree line, her foot caught on a root. Gravity took hold of her, pulling her down to the ground. Then everything went dark.

CHAPTER SIXTEEN

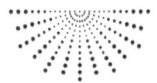

"*B*ecky? Becky, come on. Wake up."

"What was she doing out in the trees?"

"I don't know."

The voices were all familiar, even if they seemed to be all jumbled up. Becky became aware of the darkness and saw a tiny pin of light at the farthest end of it. She wanted to be in that light. Getting to it felt like she was swimming, but finally everything started to flicker into focus. Her eyes popped open, but she immediately shut them again.

"Yikes. Who is shining that spotlight on me?" She raised her hand to cover her eyes.

"Are you all right?" She knew that accent

instantly. Pushing the pain aside, Becky looked up and saw she was in Adam's big strong arms.

"I am now," she purred, but a sharp ache in the front of her head made her wince. When she reached up, she felt the pain.

"You've got a real goose egg there," Adam said.

"My gosh, Becky, what were you doing outside?" Martha asked, handing her a flask she pulled from her purse.

Becky took it, flipped the top, and took a quick swallow. The brandy felt good going down, clearing her head and bringing everything into focus.

"I needed a little air," she said, pulling herself up.

"You gotta get her outta here." Hank looked down at Becky. She was in the kitchen, where the poker games had taken place. There was no sign of any games going on now. "I'm sorry, doll, but the boss will have a kitten if an ambulance shows up here."

"I'm fine," Becky said, reluctantly pushing herself up and away from Adam. Her head swam, but she fought the sensation off with another sip of brandy.

"You screamed," Adam said. "If you hadn't, no one would have known you were out there. You could have died."

"What were you doing out there?" Becky asked, suddenly suspicious.

"Just as I got here, I saw you walking to the tree line," Adam replied. His forehead was wrinkled as if he were waiting for an explanation.

"Come, Becky," Teddy said, hitching his pants and shaking his head. "I think we ought to get you home."

Becky shook her head to chase out the fuzziness. Then she noticed Fanny. With her neckline plunging a little lower than Becky remembered, she was positioned rather dangerously close to Adam.

"I'm telling you, I'm fine. Just a little bump on the noggin." She looked down and saw the condition of her dress. It was dirty and had snags in it. A couple of dried leaves and a few strands of grass also clung to her. "Jeez, I look like I fell out of a boxcar."

That made her remember the hobo. Her stomach flipped, and she looked around nervously as everyone started talking at once. Hank wanted them out of there, and Martha was trying to get Teddy to wait while he headed toward the door to get the car.

"Oh, Rebecca, you poor thing," Fanny said as she stooped down, letting Hank, Teddy, and Adam get an eyeful of cleavage. "We've got to get you home. Adam, do you have your car?"

Becky suddenly felt nauseated. Maybe she had hit her head harder than she thought. No, it was the sight of Fanny and this act she was putting on. All that talk about being with a man of an ill reputation went right out the window when she looked at the man in question. What had Fanny said to him while Becky was out cold? What had he said in reply? And why was that more important than the dead body that was out just past the tree line?

"He's outside," Becky said. She suddenly felt her legs and tried to stand. "Eww, you guys laid me on this floor? It's grimy and dirty."

"What were we supposed to do?" Martha asked.

"I don't know. Find a blanket. Use Teddy's jacket," Becky snapped as she got to her feet, using Adam's big shoulder to balance herself.

"I didn't want my jacket to get dirty." Teddy frowned.

"Who is outside, Becky?" Adam asked.

"She's talking crazy," Fanny said.

"We need to go to the police," Becky said, looking at her friends.

"Hold on a minute." Hank stepped in. "We're not calling any police. I'm sorry, Becky. But you gotta take this show on the road. The boss will have my head if you don't. I'm not playing around."

Becky nodded. She didn't want to get anyone in trouble, but she was sure a dead man was in those trees. Not to mention the creepy old hobo who seemed to be popping up wherever she was. With everyone but Becky speaking at once, they followed the intimidating doorman to a back door. Hank held it open, and they all filed out.

"Should we go somewhere else?" Martha looked up at Teddy.

"I think we should take you to the hospital and have your head looked at," Adam said.

"I'm sure we could find another joint that's jumping. It's still early, and I think I only had about three drinks." Teddy shrugged.

"I'm sure we could drop Becky at the hospital. They'd probably want to keep her there for observation," Fanny said quietly to Adam as if she were relaying a secret.

Becky squinted at her. "I'm not going to see some quack. I'm going to the police. There is a dead man in those woods. He was at Martha's party, and I think he's responsible for killing Lawrence Hoolihan."

"He was at my party?" Martha suddenly stopped and stared at Becky. "You didn't say that."

"You didn't ask." Becky shook her head. She

remembered the deck of cards. They were still in her hands, although they were slightly crushed from her holding on to them so tightly. "Wait. I'll bet there are only fifty-one cards in this pack."

"What is she doing now?" Teddy whispered.

"Diggs threw these away as he was walking into the woods." She pulled the deck of cards from the pack and counted. As she suspected, there were only fifty-one cards. She had the remaining card in her possession. "I found a card on the floor where poor Lawrence… died."

"Oh, can't we just forget that night ever happened?" Fanny leaned into Adam as if she were going to faint. "I didn't see you there. I would have remembered."

"I wasn't invited," Adam replied but directed his focus on Becky. "Becky, you aren't making any sense. I'm taking you to the hospital."

"No, you're not." Becky pulled away from him and Fanny, who had somehow inched her way closer to Adam. "I'm going to the police. If I have to walk there alone."

"Come on. I'll drive you," Adam replied. "Although none of this is making any sense to me. I don't think it's a good idea."

"Neither do I, Rebecca," Fanny chimed in.

"I just don't think I can handle any further talk about Lawrence Hoolihan or his killer. I'm starting to feel like I need to go to the hospital," Martha said. "Teddy, do you mind blowing this pop stand?"

"Sorry, guys. Count us out. I'm lit enough that the police might toss me in the hoosegow. Same goes for Martha," Teddy said, giving her a playful jab in the ribs.

"Hey. I'm not nearly as lit as I have been. Or as I should be, considering what happened at my birthday party," Martha said before burping. "Excuse me."

"Adam, I really don't think you ought to be indulging Rebecca this way. I think that she should be brought straight home and..." Fanny tried to whisper to Adam.

"Come on, Becky. I'll take you to the police station. I don't think it's a good idea. But if you are set on going, I'll get you there," Adam said.

"Thanks, Adam. You sure are a swell guy." Becky looked up at him. She felt like she was seeing him for the first time all over again, and she smiled.

"Ahem. I think Rebecca should have some family with her. I'll tag along," Fanny insisted.

"You don't have to, Fanny. I'll be fine," Becky started to protest, but Adam shut her down.

"I think that's a good idea. This story is going to sound crazy enough. It might do you some good to have someone with who can vouch for you. I'm a Northerner. Some of these coppers don't trust a fella like me." Adam squeezed Becky's hand before leading her to his car. Fanny quickly grabbed his other arm and pulled herself close to him.

"I'm not sure this is a good idea," Fanny whispered into Adam's neck. "But I'm glad you're here. Rebecca would never listen to me. Maybe you can talk some sense into her."

Adam looked down at Fanny, who batted her eyes. Within minutes, everyone was in a car and heading toward their destination.

Becky nervously turned the deck of cards over and over in her hands as they pulled out of the crowded lot. Teddy and Martha headed south, but the police station in downtown Savannah was to the north. Adam didn't have the car on the road five minutes before they saw something emerge from the trees and stagger onto the road.

"What is that?" Becky shouted while pointing.

"Stop the car!" Fanny screamed.

Adam slammed on the brakes mere feet from the shadowy figure. While under a lonely streetlight, the group could see it was a big man who put his hand up toward the oncoming headlights and dropped to his knees before collapsing on the ground.

"That's Diggs!" Becky shouted before hopping out of the car.

"Becky! Wait!" Adam called after her, but she was already out of the car and creeping toward the man lying motionless on the road.

"Mr. Diggs?" Becky carefully crept up to him. "Mr. Diggs, can you hear me?"

At first, Diggs remained motionless. But a split second later, Diggs's eyes popped open. They were the only thing he appeared to be able to move until his lips started to flutter.

"Get out of here, or he'll get you, too."

Becky looked around, sure that Diggs was talking about the gunman.

"He'll whisper, and then he'll get you."

"Oh, Adam," Fanny whined. "I don't like this one bit. A lady should never be around such things. Get me out of here. Please."

"Becky, Fanny is right. Get back in the car," Adam hissed.

"Did you hear him? He's dying." Becky pointed to a pool of blood that spread out beneath the man's body and crept across the pavement. "Pick him up and put him in the car."

"What?" Adam and Fanny asked in unison.

"What, what?" Becky barked. "We can't leave this man just bleeding out here."

"He could be the man who killed Lawrence Hoolihan." Fanny shuddered. "You can't possibly be serious. Even if we wanted to pick him up, there is no room in the car. And I'm not going to wait on the side of the road like a common tramp."

"Becky, he's dead. Look at the blood. We can get help, but we've got to go," Adam insisted.

"But he just spoke…" Her voice trailed off. Adam and Fanny obviously hadn't heard him. Becky's heart jumped. She'd not had any experiences like this before in which the dead spoke to her in front of other people. And Diggs was as dead as a doornail. If only she could ask him if he killed Lawrence. But Adam was right there, and he'd think she'd lost her marbles. Not to mention Fanny being an all-too-willing witness to attest to Becky's unstable mental state.

"Whoever did this could still be lurking around," Fanny whispered. "We need to go and send help. None of us are equipped to address such a situation."

Becky didn't want to say it out loud, but Fanny was right. "Adam, how fast can you get to the police station?"

"Get back in the car, and I'll show you," he said.

Becky was in the passenger's seat just as Adam threw the car into gear and hit the gas. They swerved wildly around the body in the road and sped to the police station.

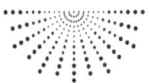

CHAPTER SEVENTEEN

"Slow down. Now tell me again what happened," Officer Fouts said as he looked skeptically at Becky and Adam before letting his eyes linger a little longer on Fanny.

"A man collapsed in the middle of the street past Woodrow Lane," Adam said. "We think he was shot."

"He *was* shot," Becky added. "And I think he is the man responsible for the murder of Lawrence Hoolihan at the Bourdeaux Estate."

"Now what do you know about the murder at the Bourdeaux place?" the officer asked, watching Becky carefully.

"I was there," Becky started. "You see, I was helping Martha Bourdeaux clean up after the festivities. It was her birthday when the man was killed.

She didn't invite Lawrence. She'd never have a fellow like that in her house, but it was her birthday, and he came along with the other fellows to play poker. See, I found this playing card, and it matched the deck that Diggs… that's the man in the street… it matched a deck he was using and—"

"You all been drinking tonight?" Officer Fouts asked. His years of experience showed in his eyes and pockmarked skin as he glared at them from behind a wooden desk covered with stacks of paper. His dark-blue uniform was as serious as his expression. Even the shiny copper buttons looked cold and grave.

"No. Of course not," Fanny piped up.

"Officer, the man was bleeding and in the middle of the street," Adam said, shifting from one foot to the other.

"Where you from, boy?" Officer Fouts asked, squinting at Adam.

Becky cleared her throat. "We had a couple of snorts, yes, but…"

"But nothing!" Officer Fouts shouted. "Where'd you get the hooch?"

"Hooch?" Fanny began to knead her hands.

"Officer, the man in the road killed—"

"I'm not playing games, missy," Officer Fouts

said. "You three have two choices. You can either tell me where you got the hooch from, or you can get out of my station with your cockamamie story before I arrest you for public intoxication."

"But we aren't drunk. Honest." Fanny batted her lashes, but Officer Fouts clearly wasn't falling for it.

Before Becky could retell her story to Officer Fouts, a mob of drunks poured into the station. Several policemen dove into the group, attempting to pull them off one another. There were flappers who were kicking and screaming, a couple of fellas in suits, and a few more who looked like they'd been working on the docks, all throwing punches and shouting insults in one another's direction.

Adam took Becky and Fanny by the hands and dragged them out of the station. Fanny acted on the verge of tears while Becky stared at the commotion, showing her disappointment that they had to leave.

"I've had enough," Adam said, pulling her toward his car. "I'm taking you home. Get in."

Outside were officers still at the paddy wagons, pulling people out. Becky heard shouting and swearing and saw some kicking and a few folks trying to bite the police and each other.

Fanny casually slid into the front seat instead of the rumble seat and looked at Becky. "Adam is right,

Becky." She patted the seat, motioning for Becky to slip in, which would ensure Fanny was in the middle and quite close to Adam for the ride home.

"We can't go home. That man is lying in the street. He's the killer," Becky insisted. "We have to go back."

"Don't get sore, Beck. But that guy on the road was whacked for a reason. The dropper could still be out there. If he sees us snooping around, who knows what kind of trouble—"

"No, Adam. I saw him drive away." Becky looked around at the commotion, which was starting to die down. She felt as frustrated and out of control as the people being bustled into the police station. The air was heavier than it had been. There was an electric smell, like a lightning storm was on the horizon. And Becky was sure something was causing her to feel jittery deep down in her chest, like standing too close to the tracks when a train was approaching. Before she could say another word to Adam, her eyes locked with the man slithering out of the paddy wagon. It was the same hobo from the poker game and the woods.

"How can you be sure it was the same guy? Maybe it was just some hack dropping off a fare. It was dark. You can't be sure what you saw," Adam said.

"Rebecca, it's getting late, and I think you should let Adam take you home," Fanny said from the car.

"It's him," Becky whispered, narrowing her eyes as she stared. "He was in the woods. When I was there, he was in the woods."

"Who?" Adam asked.

"Him. Over there." Becky pointed at the open paddy wagon. "Look. He's slipping away. The police don't see him. That man had something to do with Diggs. I just know it. Hey! Hey, stop that guy!" Becky shouted as she took a few steps closer to the commotion.

"What guy? Who are you talking about, Becky?" Adam looked at the back of the police wagon, but he didn't see anyone. The wagon was empty. The police herded everyone inside.

"That guy there! Stop..." She stared at the sinister hobo, who smiled and winked at her. "Uh... um..."

The reality fell on top of her. Adam didn't see him because he was a spirit. But he wasn't like the spirits she encountered at the cemetery. They were pleasant. Even the grouchy ones had something endearing about them. This was different. As Becky watched, the bum slipped backward into the shadows, blending into them as if he dissolved into the darkness.

Becky stopped and felt the heat of embarrassment rise up her body and ignite her cheeks. Why didn't she realize that the man wasn't a man at all? What was she doing trying to get everyone to see him when she should have known he was invisible? With a new kind of fear, she looked up at Adam. He was staring at her with such a worried face that Becky wanted to cry. Then she looked at Fanny, who looked like she was envisioning Becky in a straitjacket.

"Beck, I'm going to take you to the hospital. You must have hit your head harder than you think," Adam said.

"No. I'm all right. Maybe someone slipped me a mickey." Becky rubbed her head. "Just take me home."

"That's the first thing you've said that made any sense," Fanny interrupted. "Adam, please get her in the car. She needs rest."

"Someone will find the man, Diggs, on the road." Adam put his arm around Becky and eased her into the car. Before she could suggest going back to the club, Adam had the car in gear and headed in the direction of her home.

"I'll never forget this night," Fanny said. "I had plenty of exciting evenings when I was in Paris but nothing like this."

"You were in Paris?" Adam asked pleasantly.

What is he doing? Becky's temper stormed inside her. *Why is he goading her? What could he possibly care that she was in Paris?*

"Oh, yes. I took an extensive trip with Granny Louise. It was terribly exciting," Fanny continued.

"I'll bet it was. What was your favorite part?" Adam asked.

Becky wanted to slap them both. But just as she turned to glare at Adam, they hit a pothole. The entire car lurched, and Fanny whooped, scooting herself even closer to Adam.

This was not how she had hoped the evening would turn out. After the argument with her mother, Becky debated staying at home. But Kitty had laid out her dress in a gesture of peace. And even though Becky climbed out the window to avoid her mother, she knew Kitty would be happy she wore the dress out. What was she doing fretting over what her mother thought at a time like this? She'd seen a man get shot in the road. That man, she was sure, killed Lawrence Hoolihan, and no one believed her. As she went to run her hand through her hair, she winced as her hand grazed the lump on her forehead. That would be a bear to explain tomorrow.

After what felt like hours, they reached the dirt road that was the Mackenzie plantation drive leading to the house.

"You'd better not come up to the house," Becky blurted. "We'll get out here."

"What?" Adam asked.

"Oh, no. I can't walk all that way," Fanny tittered. "I'll just ruin my shoes."

"Have you forgotten about Kitty and Judge? They wouldn't take too kindly to a Yankee bringing us home. Old prejudices die hard, Adam. You might not be aware of that, but here in the South, we remember the War of Aggression as if it happened only a decade ago," Becky spat as she stepped out of the car. Her own shoes were ruined already. She didn't give a flying fig about Fanny's.

"A Yankee?" Adam looked at Becky.

Her heart ached inside, and all she wanted to do was cry, but her pride wouldn't let her. "That's right. Remember, Fanny, you said associating with the wrong man wouldn't just ruin my reputation but theirs."

"Well, uh, that was before I got to know Mr. White." Fanny looked at Adam and batted her eyelashes. "I do believe she's upset due to the unsightly knob on her noggin. But I did so enjoy making your acquaintance. I hope to see you again soon."

"Yes, you can tell me more about Paris," Adam said with a smile, but his eyes shifted to Becky's. "Are you sure you don't want me to drive you to the door?"

"Quite." Becky snapped and started walking up the drive. She didn't think anything could be harder than leaving Adam sitting there. No kiss goodnight. No longing look into his eyes. But the worst was that she was sure Diggs was responsible for Lawrence's death. And she was sure she saw him dealing at the poker game when that filthy little man whispered in his ear. And after she fell off the barstool, she followed him into the woods, where a real person shot him with a real gun. But that old filthy hobo was there. He had something to do with it. Yet no one but her could see him.

Behind her, Becky could hear Fanny whispering and giggling something to Adam but she couldn't hear his reply. Not until she was several yards ahead did she hear Fanny calling out to her.

"Becky! Wait for me! I can't manage in this dirt with these heels. Oh, I got these shoes in Paris. I just know they are going to be ruined," she tittered and then shouted another good-bye to Adam.

As Adam's car drove away, Becky felt her heart get dragged along with it. The feeling prompted her to quicken her pace and reach the house long before Fanny. Instead of going in through the front door, she kicked off her shoes, pulled off her dirty and torn stockings, and scaled the lattice to her open bedroom window.

Once inside her sanctuary, she wanted to throw herself down on her pillow and cry.

But she didn't. Instead, she pulled out the deck of cards and began a game of solitaire. She needed to think. Maybe something would come to her if she shuffled a dead man's deck of cards.

CHAPTER EIGHTEEN

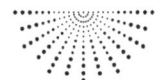

everal days had passed since the events at Willie's. Trying to conceal it with a swoop of hair for the past few days had been a real drag. Becky didn't look like herself or feel like herself. No matter what she tried to do, she couldn't shake the strange sensation that she had a cobweb brushing across her shoulders every couple of minutes when she was alone. That caused a real problem since Becky wanted to be alone.

During the day, she avoided just about everyone and took her sketchbook to the cemetery. She doodled her pictures and collected a few tombstone rubbings. But not until she decided to draw the creepy hobo did something in her mind click.

"Madame Cecelia. I can't believe I'm saying this,

but maybe she'd have some insight." The idea was a little awkward, since Becky had left that strange apartment with a rather haughty attitude. "I'll bring a gift." She snapped her fingers. But just as she was about to turn and go beg Teddy for the use of his car, she froze. Again, her spine tingled with the sensation of being watched.

Then she saw something more hideous than the dirty old bum who grinned his rotten grin at her.

"Rebecca, your mama said you'd be back here," Fanny huffed as she walked through the grass. She was like a tightrope walker at the circus trying not to step on the flat tombstones or let one of the monuments brush up against her. "This is a rather morbid environment, isn't it?"

"Is that what you came to tell me, Fanny?"

"No. I wanted to talk to you." Fanny looked around after Becky took a seat on the nearest lawn crypt. Fanny's superstitious nature obviously didn't immediately permit her to sit on a gravestone like her cousin, but it was her only option.

"What is so important, Fanny?"

"Well, your mother and I were having a lovely talk this morning, and we've decided that it would be in the best interest of everyone that I stay on here at the Mackenzie plantation for another month."

Whether Fanny wanted to admit it or not, Becky was sure that this sudden change in plans had something to do with Adam.

"Doesn't Granny Louise have travelling plans for you? Aren't you just dying to go back to Paris?" Becky held her sketchbook close to her chest like a shield from Fanny's nastiness.

"Aunt Kitty thinks that I would be a positive influence on you." Fanny lifted her chin proudly. "And I can tell you right now, Rebecca, that a young lady who hangs her hat around a saturnine place like this is not the kind of lady any man would care to take seriously. In fact, I do believe that you are sending the wrong message to many of the fellas who I've witnessed you with."

"What are you talking about? Just because you were a wallflower at Willie's and I know half the gents there doesn't mean I'm insinuating anything other than that I like to dance. What did you tell Mama?" Becky glared at her cousin, who began to stutter.

"I'm just looking out for you, Rebecca." Fanny folded her arms across her chest.

"What did you tell her?"

Fanny looked past Becky for a minute as if something had demanded her attention. She was clearly trying to think of something a little less harsh than the truth. "I told her that it was rather surprising how all the men seemed to know your name. That's all."

Becky's mouth fell open. "That's all? Fanny, you know exactly what a vague statement like that is going to sound like to my mother!"

"There is no need to shout." Fanny stood. "Perhaps *you* should think of how it looks to your poor mother. You have to admit that it would explain why no proper men want to come calling. Don't throw an ing-bing over it."

Becky abruptly stood, making Fanny jump and take a step backward. "You think you've put me in a real jam, don't you, Fanny? Boy, you are one slick number." She started to walk past her cousin but stopped short. "Did you tell Mama who drove us home the other night?"

Fanny's face went red.

"That horrible Yankee that *you* were snuggling against," Becky practically growled. "That same horrible beast that you said had a no-good reputation."

"I was just being sociable. I have no interest—"

"Ha! We'll see about that." Becky marched off, leaving Fanny to make her way gingerly through the cemetery on her own. When she arrived at the back porch, she saw Lucretia handing Moxley a piece of paper.

"Don't forget my molasses like you done last time," she scolded.

"Enough, woman. A man makes one mistake, and he pays for the rest of his life," Moxley replied as he looked in Becky's direction. "Well, hello, Miss Becky. Did Miss Fanny find you? She was looking high and low for you this morning."

"Yes," Becky grumbled as she jerked her thumb over her shoulder. "She's back there, bringing up the caboose. Say, Moxley. Are you going into town?"

"I am. Seems the world will come to an end if'n I don't get some molasses." He looked sideways at Lucretia, who replied with a harrumph and stomped back inside.

"Can I hitch a ride with you?" Becky pleaded, looking over her shoulder only to see Fanny quickly making her way past the trees and brush.

"Of course." Moxley smiled.

"Can we go now?" Becky pleaded, putting her hands together as if in prayer.

"Let's make tracks," Moxley said, sweeping his arm ahead of him for Becky to go on. She hurried to the car and hopped in the passenger seat. Within seconds Moxley had it cranked and started jostling down the dirt road in the direction of town.

"Miss Becky, do you remember when I taught you how to drive?" Moxley asked, sitting as straight as an arrow behind the steering wheel.

"I do, Moxley." Becky smiled.

"So, when you goin' to ask your father to let you drive again? I know you know how." Becky had never heard Moxley even so much as raise his voice. That was what made it almost impossible not to do what he asked.

"Why would I go do a thing like that? Have you seen the tomato plants that your little Teeter planted? They are really growing." Becky looked straight ahead.

"Now, Miss Becky, don't you go changing the subject. You just had a little mishap. They happen. I know if you asked your father, he'd loosen his punishment," Moxley said.

"I don't want to talk about this, Moxley. I'll talk to Daddy in my good time." She cleared her throat. "Besides, with Fanny staying on another month, I'm sure I won't be allowed five minutes in the water closet without her or Mama wanting to know what I'm doing."

Moxley chuckled.

"Ain't funny, Moxley. Ain't funny at all. Everyone thinks that Fanny is this prize poodle and I'm just some ugly old bulldog chasing my tail." These words made Moxley chuckle even more. Becky felt herself smiling and the irritation of her conversation with Fanny starting to melt away.

"Is that why you were in such a hurry to get away?" he asked.

"Yes."

"Well, don't you fret, Miss Becky. Things have a way of workin' theyself out." He nodded. "Miss Fanny won't be plaguing you forever."

Becky took a deep breath. "You're a good egg, Moxley."

"Now, I am assuming you have some kind of business to tend to downtown and that is why you wanted to tag along?" he asked.

"I can't fool you, can I?"

"No, Miss Becky. Do you think you'll get it wrapped up in an hour?" he asked seriously.

"Yes. Most definitely. I'm just stopping to visit a friend. Well, she's more of an acquaintance. I need to ask her something. It doesn't make a lot of sense. It seems like nothing is making sense these days. But I'm hoping she can help me sort a few things out,"

Becky said while picking at the corner of her sketchbook.

"All right. Meet me at the bank in one hour," Moxley ordered.

"I won't be a minute late," Becky said.

When Becky made it to the peculiar apothecary where Madame Cecelia and her mother resided, she was shaking. Just as she was about to barge into the shop, the door opened.

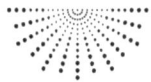

CHAPTER NINETEEN

"*T*ook you long enough, girlie-girl," Madame Cecelia's mother said, even her dead white eye glaring at Becky.

"What is your name?" Becky asked with her lips pulled into a frown.

"Ophelia," the old woman grumbled.

"Well, Ophelia, I'm behind the eight ball, and I'm afraid pretty soon someone..." Becky swallowed hard. "Or some*thing* is going to put the screws to me but good."

"We already know. Come on inside, girl." Ophelia nodded. "Go on up those stairs, but don't touch anything!"

Becky walked to the back of the apothecary and through a curtain of beads that sparkled and shimmered. The strings made a pleasant sound as she parted them and let them fall into place, like tiny, smooth pebbles hitting the sidewalk. Along the winding staircase that led up to the apartment over the store were candles illuminating statues and paintings of various saints.

Carefully, Becky made her way to the top landing and knocked on the door. She still felt tremendous energy from the apartment, but it wasn't as overwhelming as it had been the first time she arrived. Becky didn't feel at all like fainting.

"You do realize that you almost got yourself killed the other night, don't you?" These words came immediately out of Madame Cecelia's mouth when she opened the door before Becky could knock on it.

"Yes. But how did you know?" Becky asked as she entered the apartment. The smell of incense and strong coffee was comforting.

"I saw it in the cards." She shut the door behind Becky and walked to the kitchenette. Madame Cecelia wore a paisley printed skirt in rust and gold colors with a thick black beaded belt and a billowy shirt. Her long black hair hung wildly down her back in tight ringlets that were held away from her face by a bright-green scarf.

"Why didn't you warn me?"

"You didn't want me to," Madame Cecelia said as she pulled a chair out from the small table that seated four by the open window. Outside on the fire escape were some laundry hanging and a couple of flowering plants in big pots. Becky took a seat before Madame Cecelia placed a cup of steaming black coffee in front of her.

"Are you going to read the grounds once I've finished?" Becky didn't know why she felt like being a smart aleck to her hostess. After all, it was Becky who barged in on her, not the other way around.

"No. I already know your future. You're going to die," Madame Cecelia said as she took a seat across the table. "Cream or sugar?"

Becky choked down her first sip and began to cough while shaking her head. "What kind of thing is that to say? When? By who?"

Madame Cecelia started to laugh. "I'm just kidding. Oh, I mean, you *are* going to die. We all are eventually. I just said that to sort of break the ice."

"Break the ice?" Becky snapped. "You're off your nut. That's plain to see."

Madame Cecelia pointed at Becky's sketchbook and pencils that she'd brought with her. "Have you brought something to show me?"

Becky took a sip of coffee and let the hot liquid

roll down her throat and calm her nerves. She took a deep breath and started to tell Madame Cecelia about the incident outside Willie's.

"I know the man was dead. We left him there in the street. Had he seen me or worse, the pal who shot him, I'd be dead in those trees, and no one would know where I was." Becky trembled. "The police didn't believe me. They thought I was drunk and were ready to throw me in the pokey."

"And your friends?" Madame Cecelia asked, even though Becky was sure she already knew the answer.

"They didn't believe I saw what I saw. They said it was better to stay out of the mob's business. But that guy, Diggs, killed Lawrence Hoolihan. He was at Martha's party. He was dealing poker, and Adam said the guy had a bad rep as a Johnson brother. A real criminal," Becky said before taking another sip of coffee.

"What makes you think he's your man?" Madame Cecelia asked.

"He was at the scene. I found a card from his deck of cards lying on the floor where the body was found. It's kind of a crazy coincidence, don't you think?" asked Becky.

"I'm going to tell you right now that Diggs wasn't

your guy." Madame Cecelia looked at Becky with blazing green eyes.

"But you just said I almost got myself killed the other night. That was because I was following Diggs." Becky worried the spot on her forehead where she'd had the goose egg.

"No. There was something far worse there looking for you," Madame Cecelia said. "Whatever he is, he's always on the lookout for you."

"Wait." Becky picked up her sketchbook and flipped several pages over before she found the image she wanted.

Madame Cecelia gasped when she saw the pencil sketch of a wrinkled old man in dirty, worn clothes with leering eyes and a rotten smile. "Where did you see that?"

"Why? Who is it?" Becky asked.

"Not who. What." Madame Cecelia took a sip of her coffee and stared at the image while leaning back in her seat. She acted as if she were afraid it might jump off the page at her.

"I saw him. It was at Willie's dance hall, and then he was coming out of the paddy wagon when we went to the police to tell them about Diggs getting shot," Becky replied. "No one saw him but me. I tried to get Adam to look, but he thought I was having visions due to the bump on my head." Her hand went to the spot on her forehead, which was much smaller but still there and still tender.

Madame Cecelia rose from her seat. She walked over to a tall, slender bookcase and ran her finger along the spines of several thick, aged books before finally settling on one. She pulled a maroon-colored tome that was about an inch thick off the shelf and slowly returned to her seat at the small table, her eyes scanning the pages quickly. When she found what she was looking for, she set the book down. "Read this."

Becky looked down at the page. She had expected to see a drawing of a creature similar to what she'd drawn. But nothing was there but a short couple of lines in fancy black script on pages that were as thin as tissue. Carefully, Becky leaned forward and read the words:

"Keep alert when in the presence of vice. The instigator will be there and can take you willingly or unwillingly deeper into that world." With interest, she leaned closer and continued to read. "It is with ignorance people assume they make their own choices autonomously, as there is always a figure whispering in their ear the rewards of each decision."

Madame Cecelia leaned back on her heels, and Becky looked up at her.

"I don't follow," Becky admitted.

"You've had the gift of communicating with the dead, I'm guessing, since you can remember. That's what I've been told," Madame Cecelia said flatly.

"Who told you? If Teddy spilled the beans after too many sips of Aunt Rue's special ambrosia, I'm going to box his ears," Becky huffed.

"No. It wasn't Teddy. Actually, I could see them flock to you the second you arrived. You saw my family around me as well while we were standing on the porch at Martha's party." Madame Cecelia winked.

"So you can talk to them too?" Becky asked carefully. Part of her was hoping Madame Cecelia would say yes and offer some kind of guidance or instruction about what she was supposed to do with this specific talent. But another part of Becky wanted the Gypsy to say no so her gift would still be unique, a mystery and totally hers.

"Yes. I had to tell them all to stay back when you arrived today. You remember what happened last time. It was like beer spilled in the streets the way they came at you." The madame took a sip of her coffee.

"Yes. I remember that all too well."

"If it's any consolation, they all think you are the cat's pajamas. Except for Cousin Mimi. That explains why my mother likes you so much. Those two will be at odds until the end of time." Madame Cecelia leaned back in her chair and folded her arms. Her bright-red nails glistened like the polish was still wet. "But when you placed your hand on that Ouija board at Martha Bourdeaux's party, you threw open a door that will be near impossible to shut."

"So what am I supposed to do? What about this gent?" Becky tapped on the face of her drawing.

"He's a messenger of sorts. Like the passage you read said, there is a whisperer. I'll bet where you saw him, you were in the presence of some unorthodox goings-on." Madame Cecelia leaned forward.

"When I first saw him, he was at the poker game. He just appeared out of nowhere," Becky said. "Then he was in the woods, and that was what caused me to hit my head. And then I saw him at the police station with all the rummies while the brawl was spilling out of the paddy wagon."

"Sound like he keeps lovely company," Madame Cecelia replied.

"But he isn't a dead man. So why do I see him?"

Becky pushed her coffee cup away from her and folded her arms on the table.

"I think he came through that spirit board and has found that Savannah is the perfect city for his kind of mischief." Madame Cecelia flipped her hair behind her shoulders.

"When I decided to take a jaunt up here and see you, I was sure I'd get some answers. But Madame Cecelia, you have caused me to realize I am more confused than I was an hour ago. Good heavens, what time is it?" Becky stood up.

"Ten to one," the Gypsy said.

"Fine. I'm not too late. I've got to be running, or Moxley will box my ears for making him wait." Becky extended her hand. "I do appreciate you talking to me, even though you were very little help and added to my confusion."

"Anytime, Becky. I told you that you have friends here." Madame Cecelia smiled.

"Speaking of friends, whatever happened to Count Ernesto? Did he head back to Transylvania or Romania or wherever you guys are from?" Becky teased as she made her way to the door.

"He's at work. You don't think we all just hang around telling fortunes all day, do you?" She winked. "He works at the newspaper."

"Of course he does. That's how your mother knew about Adam. Why, that sneaky so-and-so," Becky muttered as she imagined Adam White and his new admirer, Fanny, fawning all over him.

"When you go downstairs, my mother has something for you. Take it, whatever it is." Madame Cecelia nodded.

"Your mother told me her name is Ophelia. That's a pretty name," Becky said as she stepped onto the stair landing. "Thanks for the coffee."

While Becky wound her way down the stairs, she tried to organize her thoughts. Even though she still felt confused, she also felt that a weight had been lifted from her.

"That's probably because misery loves company," she muttered but wished she hadn't when she saw Ophelia standing at the apothecary door, holding it open with a scowl on her face.

"You don't have to feel like only the dead can be trusted," Ophelia scolded. "We've invited you into our home, and you still don't trust us? Here. Maybe this will help convince you that we are genuine." She handed Becky a small velvet box and a thin paper bag.

Becky peeked in the bag to see another pair of stockings. "How did you know I needed these?"

The old woman pinched her mouth together and cocked her milky eye at Becky. "What girl doesn't need a new pair of stockings?" A smile tickled at the corners of her lips as she started to laugh at her own joke.

Becky smirked and opened the little velvet case. Her eyebrows shot up, and she suddenly felt a wave of guilt for passing such harsh judgment on the Gypsy and her mother.

"I can't take this. It's beautiful, but I can't take it." Becky stuttered as she admired a sparkling silver cuff bracelet. She could see her reflection in the massive purple stone set in the middle of a filigree design that wrapped tightly around her wrist. The bracelet had small points of silver that hugged Becky's wrist as if it were custom-made for her.

"You borrow it. Bring it back when you are done," Ophelia said, closing the little box in Becky's hand.

"When I'm done?"

"Yes. And if you don't, I will put a curse on you and your whole family that will make the plagues of Moses's time look like a Sunday picnic." Ophelia gasped but could only keep a straight face for a few seconds before she started to chuckle. "Don't be such a flat tire. You bring it back when you are done with it."

Becky rolled her eyes before thanking Ophelia, leaving the apothecary, and hurrying in the direction of Moxley's bank. She held her treasures close to her as she wove in and out of the crowds, crossing the street against the light and getting honked and yelled at by angry drivers.

Moxley was just emerging from the bank when Becky arrived. "Right on time," Becky said as she sashayed up to him, smiling.

"Lucky for you. If I let Lucretia wait any longer for her molasses, I'm afraid you might be walking home," Moxley said as he held the back door open for Becky to climb in the back seat. He took his seat in front and began to chatter to Becky about something. She wasn't paying too much attention as she admired the pretty bauble Madame Cecelia and Ophelia had given her.

"Loaned," she muttered, wondering what they meant by keeping it until she was done with it. The bracelet was beautiful. She didn't think she'd ever be done with it.

"What's that, Miss Becky?" Moxley asked.

"Oh, nothing, Moxley. I'm just thinking out loud."

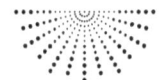

CHAPTER TWENTY

That evening, the police stopped by the Mackenzie plantation for a second chance to talk to everyone who had been at Martha's party. From what Becky could tell, they hadn't made much progress. But after she spoke with them, she was sure they might have thought she had something to do with it.

"Did you find the body of Mr. Diggs near Willie's club?" she whispered to Officer Hamilton, who sweated terribly beneath his uniform in the evening heat.

"How do you know about that?" he asked, tugging at his collar.

"I went to the station to report it. I must say that a lady isn't taken very seriously when she comes to report a murder. Officer Fouts threatened to incarcerate me for suggesting Mr. Diggs had something to do with the death of Lawrence Hoolihan." She cleared her throat, straightening her back as she peered behind the officer to make sure Kitty and Judge were not within hearing distance.

"What makes you think he did it?" Officer Hamilton asked. He had a round face and thinning hair that was slicked down across the top of his head.

As Becky explained her theory and the discarded playing cards, she found the officer's expression of mild annoyance to be, well, annoying.

"Wouldn't you agree that it's rather suspicious to find the missing card from his deck in the room where the body was found?" she asked with a shrug.

"I think Paul Diggs crossed the wrong guy and got fit for a Chicago overcoat. He had a rep of being a petty hood, but he was no killer," Officer Hamilton said. "Young lady, if I may suggest something…"

Becky nodded and leaned closer.

"Leave the crime solving to the professionals. Savvy?"

"Well, no need to be a Bruno about it. I can take a hint." Becky flipped her hair and turned to join her father, who was standing on the porch, puffing his pipe and staring off across the tobacco fields. When she looked over her shoulder, she caught the officer taking a good long drink of Fanny as she sauntered by.

"Why, this whole mess has had me in knots for the longest time. Are you any closer to catching the person who did this?" she purred to Officer Hamilton, whose expression did a one-eighty and became as pleasant as punch when Fanny spoke to him.

"We're doing the best we can, miss. Don't you worry." He flashed a goofy, toothy grin.

"I was the first one to discover the body. As I told your partner over there, I'd just returned from Paris and was in quite a state. That isn't the kind of homecoming a girl like me is used to," Fanny continued.

"I'll bet not," Officer Hamilton stuttered. Becky shook her head and planted herself next to her father.

"I never asked you what you think of all this. Who do you think did poor old Lawrence Hoolihan in?" Becky slipped her hand through the crook of her father's arm.

"I'm more concerned about what's happening in my own house." He puffed pensively, looking down and sideways at Becky, who instantly felt a twinge of guilt in her chest. She knew what he was referring to.

"Oh, Daddy. It just seems like no one trusts me to do anything right. Just because I get my dresses torn and dirty doesn't mean I'm some kind of loon," Becky said. "Nor am I anything like Fanny has made me out to be. You believe me, don't you, Daddy?"

He pulled his pipe from his mouth. The sweet-smelling smoke swirled around his head. "I know you are a bright and resourceful young lady. I also know that you are a bit on the wild side. That's not always fittin' for a Southern belle."

"Ugh, I'm more like a Southern gong, Daddy, and you know it."

Judge's belly shook as he chuckled. "That might very well be. But it's no excuse to go upsetting your mama."

Becky furrowed her brow and stood on her tiptoes to whisper harshly in her father's ear, "I'm not the one upsetting her. Miss Fanny Nosy-Britches is." She fell back to her heels and crossed her arms in front of her.

"Be that as it may, I know your mama doesn't like you giving her the cold shoulder. She's the only mama you got. Unlike Miss Fanny Nosy-Britches, who has everyone and their mother looking out for her." Judge put his pipe back in his mouth and puffed.

"Mama wishes I was like Fanny. She said as much. I never in my life said anything so cruel to her." Becky pouted. "Doesn't she think that I might have liked Mrs. Santa Claus or maybe the Tooth Fairy to be my mama? I could have. But I never said it."

Again, Judge's belly jiggled. "Ever since you were born, your mama has fretted over you, Rebecca. She worries every day. She wants you to be healthy and well taken care of. No different from any other mama worth her salt."

"She wants me to be something I'm not. I'm strange, Daddy." Becky looked out at the tobacco fields. "I can't help it. The good Lord made me odd, and I'm doing my best to cover it up, but you know what the song says. Don't hide it under a bushel."

"Rebecca, you do say the funniest things." Judge shook his head.

"Daddy, is it true that Fanny is staying on another month?" Becky slipped her hand into her father's and squeezed it.

"I'm afraid it is. Seems that she was supposed to go to Cousin Felicity's ranch in Otswego, Kansas, but they suddenly came up with a bout of pox or fever or heaven knows what." He looked down at his daughter. "I think they suffer from the same affliction you do. They just don't like her."

"How can that be? I thought everyone adored Fanny." Becky rolled her eyes.

"I'll tell you what it is. Cousin Felicity's daughter Maxine is getting married, and the last thing they want is Fanny prancing around her beau, throwing cold water on his feet," Judge replied quietly.

Now it was Becky's turn to giggle.

"Do me a favor, darlin'. Go on and talk to your mama. Do it for me," Judge said as he tilted his head to the right. "I don't ask you for too much, do I?"

Becky's shoulders sagged. She looked up at the roof over the porch and focused on a spider web that was white and wispy in the corner. She tried to think of something to say that would get her out of talking to her mother, at whom she was still angry. Of course, she'd talk to her sooner or later. But she just didn't want to now. Not yet.

"Fine." She sighed dramatically.

"That's my girl." Judge kissed the top of his daughter's head before she could turn and stomp off.

Inside the house, it was a good bit warmer. The temperature outside was well below eighty degrees, but the cool night air had yet to circulate through the house.

Kitty was sitting in her sewing room, her latest reading project in her hands as she spoke to the other officer who enviously watched Officer Hamilton talk with Fanny. Becky walked along the porch and was about to enter from the French windows when she stopped to let her mother talk to the officer.

"I'm just so distressed over the whole thing. I didn't know the boy, Lawrence, you see. But nonetheless, I am just dizzy over the whole escapade," Kitty said, shaking her head.

"I do appreciate your taking the time to talk with us again, Mrs. Mackenzie," the officer said.

"Well, I do hope you find the brute who did this. It would certainly put the people who were in attendance at the party at ease," Kitty replied. "My goodness, the scandal is crippling."

Becky waited as her mother went on about the black mark this incident would leave on the Bourdeauxs' reputation. She would never say it out loud and risk her mother slipping into a coma of humiliation, but Becky would have loved the murder to have taken place in her own home. How exciting, and people would be much more interested in that than in any silly old trip to Paris.

"Aunt Kitty?" Fanny weaseled her way into the sewing room from the foyer, where she'd been standing with Officer Hamilton. "I think these gentlemen could use a cold drink before they venture back out into the world of preventing crime. Wouldn't you agree?"

"Of course, Fanny. Tell Lucretia to pour them a couple of glasses of lemonade," Kitty replied. "Where is Becky?"

"I don't know where she's run off to this time," Fanny huffed. "She left me in that creepy old cemetery this morning, and I haven't seen her since."

Becky watched her mother take a deep breath and slowly release it.

"Is there anything else I can do for you, Aunt Kitty?"

Then, something ugly caught Becky's attention. The experience was like walking through a field of high grass and stopping short of a garden spider the size of a baseball hovering chest high in its web. That had happened to Becky on more than one occasion. Just one more step, even half a step, and she would have had the eight-legged thing on her clothes, scurrying upward toward her face, her hair... oh, the horror. Becky stared in disbelief as a familiar man emerged, like a creeping spider, from the corner of the room. She knew his hunched form and his earnest shuffle. It was the dirty hobo she'd seen whispering to Diggs at the poker game, the one who had climbed out of the paddy wagon and who'd stared right at her in the woods before she slipped on a tree root and nearly killed herself.

He gave a wide smile, like at any second he would start laughing as he sidled up to Fanny, who stooped down to talk to Kitty. Without pulling his eyes from Becky's, he chuckled and whispered something in Fanny's ear.

Part of Becky wanted to jump into the room, pointing and screaming at the little troll as it whispered its poisonous secrets, but her memory of trying to convince Adam it was really there kept her quiet. All she could do was watch, recalling what Madame Cecelia had her read from that old book. This thing wasn't like the lovely Mr. Wilcox, who roamed the cemetery, telling her stories of his family and giving her nuggets of advice. This thing was *bad*.

"I'm really sorry that your daughter can't seem to find time for you. It's got to be a phase she's going through. I can't believe she's just selfish," Fanny said.

"Although I have been known to give the wrong people the benefit of the doubt."

Becky's eyes almost popped out of her skull. She took a deep breath, expecting her mother to confirm Fanny's comments.

"You don't know my daughter that well, Fanny," Kitty replied without looking at her. "If you don't mind, please ask Lucretia for that lemonade."

In no way could Becky hold back her smirk. She glared at the little man, who shook his finger at her. Perhaps smirking at him wasn't the right thing to do. He didn't respond well to being taunted.

"Rebecca!" he shouted. Spit flew from his rotten mouth, and he clenched his fists as his crooked body shook with anger. But before Becky could say anything, he disappeared just as Fanny walked from the room toward the kitchen.

The two officers almost broke their own necks watching Fanny skirt past them. The insecurity Becky felt washed over her like a wave. Every time she saw Fanny, she was reminded of how she'd clung to Adam and he'd made no effort to tell her to shove off.

"For Pete's sake," Becky muttered. Holding her breath, she walked into her mother's sewing room, tripping over the carpet in front of the window and stumbling into her mother's stationery desk.

"Oh, there you are," Kitty said. "I wondered what had happened to you."

"I've been around. I heard you've been discussing my behavior outside this house with Cousin Fanny." Becky rubbed her knee that had hit the desk before stepping up to her mother.

"I've just asked her what her opinion is of where you go and who you associate with," Kitty said, looking down at her sewing.

"I associate with Martha Bourdeaux and Teddy Rockdale, like I have for ages. Why didn't you just ask me?" Becky wrinkled her nose as if she smelled something foul. "Instead of getting your information from an outsider."

"Becky. I do think you are getting ruffled for nothing. I'm your mother. Don't I have a right to know what you are up to and who you are associating with?" Kitty looked so worried that Becky was afraid the woman might blow away like a dry leaf on a fall breeze.

"Of course, Mama. But I do wish you'd trust me. I know a lot more than you think. I'm not some rube who just fell off the turnip truck." Becky knelt in front of her mother. "For instance, having a few dances with a Yankee isn't all that scandalous. Especially when he wants to come calling like a proper gentleman, but fear of my mother's reaction has prompted me to tell him no."

Kitty smoothed her daughter's wavy red hair from her forehead. "Let's see what pans out with this horrible incident at the Bourdeauxs' house before we go on and invite trouble. Poor Leona is thinking of cancelling her anniversary party."

"What? They always celebrate their anniversary party," Becky said. At the last three celebrations, she had won a dollar and twenty cents total playing poker, was deemed the charades champ, and had danced at least once with every gent in the place without her mother noticing.

"I know. It would be a shame," Kitty said.

"That's still a couple of months off. This whole incident might blow over in a few more weeks. We don't know," Becky said encouragingly.

"You do look on the bright side of things. How hopeful you always are," Kitty said with a smile. "My, that's pretty." She pointed at the bracelet around Becky's cuff.

"Isn't it? But it snags. See, these little points are so elegant, but they catch on my clothes. Still, I think it's too pretty not to show off." Becky smiled, thinking of Madame Cecelia and Ophelia.

Just then, Fanny interrupted with a silver tray and four glasses of lemonade.

"Becky. There you are," she said with a sigh. "I'm sorry. I didn't know you were lurking about, so there are only four glasses of lemonade."

"I'm not thirsty." Becky reached for a glass and handed it to her mother. "It looks like the police are finished. Fanny, would you bring them their lemonade so they can be on their way?"

Fanny looked down at Becky and forced a smile. Obviously, she had wanted to talk to Kitty alone. After checking the corners and not finding the hobo crouched and waiting in any of them, Becky stood and smiled back at Fanny.

"Where are you going now?" Kitty asked.

"Nowhere, Mama. I've had a busy day. I think I'm going to go turn in early, as the pickers say." She kissed her mama on the cheek and headed toward the kitchen so she could avoid bumping into Fanny, who was enjoying the attention from the policemen.

"Rebecca?" her mother called.

"Yes, Mama?"

"Thank you for coming to talk to me," Kitty said, smiling.

Becky nodded and rolled her eyes as she grinned at her mother. A couple of smart replies crossed her mind, but she decided to say nothing. Her mother was a good egg, she knew. She just wished she wouldn't worry about marrying her off or making sure she "fit in" with all the snoots in town. As much as she hated to admit it, taking her father's advice and talking to her mother made her feel light again. Oh, how she hated how right he was all the time.

Just as Becky entered the kitchen, she was alerted to some very exciting news.

"Hey, Miss Becky. I found a toad," Teeter boasted as he sat in his kitchen chair, his bare feet swinging excitedly.

"You did? Is your mama gonna make soup out of him?" Becky teased.

"No, Miss Becky. I already named him."

"Oh, I see. He's already part of the family. Can't eat him now. What's his name?"

"Herman." Teeter smiled, his white teeth gleaming. "He practically jumped right up into my lap."

"Well, that sounds swell, Teeter." Becky walked up to Lucretia as she washed the dishes. "You sure you ain't making a soup out of him?" she whispered, making Lucretia chuckle quietly.

"If that boy could put a leash on a housefly and

bring it home as a pet, he would," Lucretia replied. "What you want, Miss Becky? I'll get it for you."

"No, Lucy. That's all right. I'll just help myself to a bit of this lemonade," Becky said, getting herself a glass with chips of ice before filling it to the top.

"Didn't Miss Fanny just bring some out?"

"That wasn't for me. That was for her and the policemen at the door." Becky shook her hips, making Lucretia laugh again.

"Those men are asking everyone questions. I hear they even asked Penelope what she was doin' at the time of that poor man's death." Lucretia clicked her tongue.

"I shudder to think of how Penny answered them." Becky raised her eyebrows.

"Mm-hmm. You know she don't take kindly to anyone asking her business. Those poor detectives." Lucretia continued to shake her head and click her tongue.

"I wouldn't fret over them too much," Becky replied. "They've probably dealt with tougher nuts than Penny. Not many, I'm sure. But one or two."

"My, they must be stumped something terrible over that murder at the Bourdeauxs' place. I do hope they find out who did that terrible thing," Lucretia whispered as she continued washing and stacking the dishes.

"I'm sure they will," Becky said. "There were only so many people there, and sooner or later the guilty party always makes a mistake."

"You think so, Miss Becky?"

"That's what I've heard." Becky shrugged then walked up to Teeter to give him a kiss on the head. "I'm turning in." Becky yawned and stretched before taking a long sip of lemonade.

"You sound like the pickers in the field." Lucretia smiled. "Night, Miss Becky."

"Good night, Miss Becky. Don't let the bedbugs bite!" Teeter added.

"Good night, Teeter. Tomorrow, you introduce me to Herman. I want to make sure I recognize him if I see him crossing the pond." Becky winked, making the boy grin and nod.

The cool, sweet lemonade brought a welcome chill over Becky's shoulders as she ascended the back stairs and headed to her room. But before she got there, she heard a quiet argument. As she inched her way down the hall, she quickly realized the voices were coming from her room.

"I don't care. You won't tell Becky a thing," a voice hissed.

CHAPTER TWENTY-ONE

$\mathcal{I}$n mere seconds, Becky silently crept up to her open door and peered inside. There she found Fanny at her vanity and poor Dolores looking helpless and angry as she fidgeted with the notebook in her hand. Becky instantly recognized the book as her own day journal.

"What's going on?" Becky asked, looking sternly at Dolores and Fanny.

"Oh, um, Rebecca. I thought you were downstairs with your mother," Fanny stuttered. She had quickly stood up and held something behind her back.

"What do you think you are doing?" Becky never took her eyes off Fanny, even though Dolores stood right there. The ringleader's identity was obvious. After all the years Dolores had been with the

Mackenzies, she'd never gone snooping. This was obviously Fanny's idea.

"Well... I... your mother has been very worried about you," Fanny said. "I thought if I could find something that could explain why you've been acting the way you have, something that might help put your mother's mind at ease, then it would solve everyone's problems."

"Dolores, you can leave," Becky said.

With a quick nod, Dolores handed Becky the items in her hands and then quickly shuffled out of the room, her eyes staying focused on her own feet.

"This is my day schedule," Becky said, holding the small book in her hand.

"All right. I thought that it would be important to know whom you were associating with. Granny Louise always says that you can tell a lady by the company she keeps," Fanny said. "I'm just trying to help."

"What do you have behind your back?" Becky asked.

Reluctantly, Fanny revealed one of Becky's sketchbooks. Becky snatched it out of her hand. She flipped through her familiar drawings, wondering how harshly Fanny had judged them, since most were of wildflowers and thick, heavy trees and insects she'd stumbled across in the cemetery. Some were of her ghostly friends too.

"Rebecca, I'm just worried about you. If people found out that you were so obsessed with that morose piece of property out there, why, I just don't even want to think of the rumors that…"

"You mean if you told them about my hobbies, they might turn on me and confide in you." Becky took a step closer.

"You need to watch that temper of yours." Fanny cleared her throat. "The sad truth is everyone knows already how peculiar you are. I've heard from the ladies in the beauty salon and down at the corner drug store, and even at Gimbles, the sales ladies gave your mother the once over because you weren't there with us."

Becky was shaking. It took all her strength to hold back from clobbering Fanny. That was what the girl needed: a good kick in the pants.

"Get out of my room," Becky hissed. She raised her hand and pointed to the door. The bracelet snagged on her skirt, but Becky didn't care. "And if I ever find out that you've been snooping in here or anywhere else on the Mackenzie Estate, I'll make sure Mama throws you out. You'll have to take a streetcar back to Granny Louise and explain to her how your own kin tossed you out on your ear."

Fanny squared her shoulders and headed slowly toward to the door.

"I'll leave. But remember one thing, Rebecca. You may not think much of me, but your mother does. I'm not going anywhere. And I don't plan on letting some freak who hangs around a cemetery ruin my reputation." She turned and stormed out of the room, slamming the door behind her.

Becky's jaw hit the floor. Her feet started to move before she stopped herself at her bedroom door. The urge to grab Fanny by her flowing golden locks and yank her to the ground was overwhelming. But something stopped her: not her conscience but that dirty bum who had whispered to Fanny. In real life, Fanny Doshoffer would never come within ten feet of a degenerate like that. She might click her tongue and say, "Tsk, tsk," at how sad his situation might be, but she'd never reach out to help.

"Of course, he isn't a real person," Becky said to herself often. But this time, she looked at the bedroom door and was sure that Fanny probably had her ear pressed against it.

Grabbing her sketchbook and pencils along with a flashlight she kept in the bottom drawer of her bureau, Becky decided she wanted some air. Quietly, she changed into an old worn-out pair of dungarees she wore when she helped in the fields. Her mother hated her pants because they were wide and came so high up on her waist that they needed to be tied with a twine. Becky loved them, and had it been proper, she would have worn them in the middle of Main Street with a toothpick in her mouth and a bottle of bathtub gin in her hand. But alas, that was not to be.

The police were still there on the porch with Judge, chatting quietly about the murder. Judge, who managed to keep his emotions out of the equation, told the two officers that he'd only seen one fellow in the parlor who he didn't know. As it turned out, Judge saw Diggs.

"But please understand that current laws prevent me from telling you what I was doing at the time I witnessed the stranger." Judge chuckled. All the policemen knew there was liquor at the party. Mr. Bourdeaux had paid the proper channels to ensure a good time was had by *all*. That included the local coppers. "Have you spoken to the Heathcliff boy? I know he was watching the poker game. He didn't play, as far as I saw. But perhaps he saw something."

"Yeah, Judge. We asked him and half the young people in town. It is a doggone mystery if ever there was one. No one seems to know anything," Officer Hamilton said.

"Well, good luck, boys. I'm sure you'll settle this in due time," Judge said, shaking their hands. Then they got back into their cherry topper and drove off.

Carefully, Becky shimmied down the trellis. Once her feet were on solid ground, Becky took off into the darkness toward the Old Brick Cemetery. Just going out there after Fanny had made such an issue out of it made Becky feel better.

She'd really tried to be nice to Fanny when they first met. But Fanny was one of those girls who thrived on drama. Everyone was jealous of her not because she was so beautiful but because her beauty allowed her to get away with being full of horse-feathers. That was what was so intolerable.

But Becky wasn't interested in the inner workings of Fanny Doshoffer at the moment. She snapped on the flashlight, even though she knew the trail to the cemetery by heart, and enjoyed the feeling of complete freedom of being in the dark, alone and no one knowing where she was. At least, she had assumed no one knew where she was. However, upon reaching the crumbling gate and wall of the entrance, she saw a familiar face, one she was strangely very glad to see.

CHAPTER TWENTY-TWO

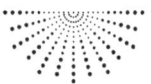

"I knew something was going to happen when the spirits led me here," Madame Cecelia said. "I don't have a lot of time. This is a warning."

"What? What are you talking about?" Becky asked as she approached. "No *hi, fancy meeting you here* or *I love what you've done with the place?*" Becky joked, but Madame Cecelia looked around nervously.

"You're in danger."

"Not here," Becky replied, sweeping her arm around her. "I'm as safe as a kitten in this place. People are so skittish and superstitious about bone-yards that I could probably walk the grounds naked and no one would ever take notice. Not that they would even if I did it in the center of town." Becky shrugged and frowned playfully.

"I'm not kidding, Rebecca. It came to me in a dream. You are in terrible danger. Are you wearing the bracelet I gave you?" She rushed toward Becky and took her hold of her hands. "You must wear it. Until I request it back."

"Well, I didn't want to risk losing it out here. And it didn't quite go with my outfit," Becky joked.

"This is no laughing matter. Rebecca, please. There is a sinister force that is quickly approaching. I'm not sure where it's come from, since Savannah, Georgia, is hardly the sleepy town city slickers like to make it. If only they could see what I see. What *we* see. Then they'd realize the truly mystical beauty that is in this city." Madame Cecelia looked around as if she were expecting an ambush at any moment.

"I'll tell you what brought that foul wind." Becky chuckled. "My cousin Fanny Doshoffer. If something offensive has blown in, you can bet she brought it with her. All the way from Paris."

"Rebecca, have you seen that man again? The one you showed me the picture of? He's close by, isn't he?" Madame Cecelia asked.

Becky wasn't sure what to say. She could lie and say, "No, haven't seen the bugger since that day after

Willie's speakeasy at the police station." All she'd wanted was a little quiet to smell the goldenrod and feel the cool breeze as the crickets chirped. The moon was just a fingernail in the sky, and the stars twinkled happily. It was a beautiful night to be out. It was a horrible night to get warnings and riddles.

"Yeah," Becky replied slowly, shining her flashlight on the ground around Madame Cecelia's feet.

"He's managed to find a way into your house, hasn't he?"

"What do you mean? He's just a spook. One of these spirits that's hanging around." Becky was really trying to convince herself that was all the little man was. She'd seen ghosts outside of the cemetery before. Why, Teeter's grandfather used to amuse him in his bassinette shortly after he was born and would be out with Lucretia when she hung laundry. Gerty Feebles had her brother, who was killed in the Great War—World War I, that is, not the Civil War—follow behind her every time she went shopping with her mother and when Gerty would meet Brian Tucker for a soda. Becky could see them, down to the tiniest freckle or the slightest facial tick. They were around, and they were real, and they never so much as said boo to her. That old hobo was no different.

"He's not. And you know this." Madame Cecelia squinted as she studied Becky's face in the dim light from the flashlight. "He has more to do with the death of that boy in the Bourdeauxs' house than you know."

"Well, what's his name? Can you tell me that? Did you see it in some tea leaves or something? I'll go to the police with it, and maybe things can get back to normal around here," Becky snapped.

"You know it doesn't work that way, Rebecca. You of all people know." Cecelia sounded annoyed.

"Say I believe you." Becky cleared her throat. "You *are* standing here in my cemetery. I don't think you would have traveled all this way on a goose chase. It is obvious you are determined that I accept this fact that the dirty little man who whispers in people's ears is more than a spook. What can I do about it? I can't stop him any more than I can stop Mr. Wilcox from coming to visit, or the lady from the Civil War who makes fun of my clothes, or the little girl who likes to see my drawings. Even if I could somehow get them to go, I don't think I would. The same goes for the bum."

"He's not just a spook! He's much more dangerous than that. He's—"

"Look, Madame Cecelia, I came out here to get a

little quiet. Now it feels like Count Basie's Orchestra is pounding away in my head," Becky whined.

"You silly little girl! I'm trying to help you! That *little hobo* is unlike anything you've ever dealt with, and if you don't protect yourself, he's going to worm his way into your house and your head, and then your gift... it'll become his!" Madame Cecelia shouted. Some of the nearby crickets halted their serenade.

Becky didn't take kindly to being shouted at. In all her years here on Earth, she could count on one hand how many people had raised their voice to her, and in each instance, those people were related to her by blood. No one else dared. After growing up seeing ghosts, there wasn't a whole lot Becky Mackenzie feared. And that included Madame Cecelia.

"Rebecca, please. I've come to warn you about..."

"I don't want to hear any more," Becky replied calmly.

"Ever since you touched that Ouija board, it's like you lit a torch, letting them, letting *him* know where you are. He doesn't like that you can see him, and he's going to use any means necessary to hurt you. Maybe even kill you." Madame Cecelia folded and unfolded her hands nervously.

"If he wants my gift, what good would I be dead?" Becky smirked. She thought she'd caught Madame Cecelia in a trick.

"Your gift would be gone. He'd inherit it only to use it for wickedness. These *spooks* you talk to, the little girl who enjoys your drawings, she'd come to him. Judging by what you know and feel about him now, what do you think he'd do to that little spirit? Do you really think he'd sit and show her pictures and talk to her? Of course you don't. You might be stubborn, but you are not stupid."

"And what would you have me do about it?" Becky asked through clenched teeth.

"I think I have a spell that might get him to leave. But it will cost—"

"Oh! Oh, now I get it!" Becky let out a bitter chuckle, rolled her eyes, and took a few steps away from the fortune-teller. "It *is* some kind of flimflam. This is how you make your money. Find someone dumb Dora gullible enough to believe your phonus-bolonus and then sink them for every nickel you can, selling cheap charms and magic powders. Well, sorry, toots, but I know my onions, and you aren't going to make a chump out of me."

"No. You're wrong."

"Save it for your Aunt Tilly," Becky spat as she

turned and started walking back to the house. Madame Cecelia called after her once, but Becky didn't look back. She thought back to her visits to the apothecary and Ophelia's home. She'd probably just gotten a whiff of some weird incense that made her woozy that first time. Gypsies like them couldn't be trusted. Becky learned her lesson the hard way.

But they gave you that bracelet. Why would they give you something so pretty for free and then expect you to pay for their dried dandelions and tobacco from a ciggy like it was some kind of magic mixture? Becky's mind fought to find a reasonable answer. Either she believed Madame Cecelia was really trying to help, or she didn't. As she shimmied up the trellis back to her room, she decided she didn't believe the woman. However, everything she'd said stayed with her, gnawing at her brain and keeping her up well past midnight.

Finally, sleep overcame Becky. But it wasn't the peaceful, dark sleep that enveloped her most nights. It was a sketchy, exhausting sleep that woke her up over and over again with vivid dreams that repeated Madame Cecelia's words like a record skipping. When Becky finally woke up the next day, even Lucretia's strong black coffee didn't clear her head.

And so it went for several nights. Becky volunteered for chores around the house. She accompanied Moxley to town, making sure to steer clear of Madame Cecelia's apothecary but happy to run from one end of the shopping district to the other for her mother and even Fanny. She went to the cemetery, where she roamed listlessly. Since the murder at Martha's place, the opportunity to visit any of the swinging clubs had died down for Becky. Of course, she didn't expect to go out every night of the week, but it had been almost ten days, and no one had offered any invitations. Becky was getting so desperate that she considered joining her mother for one of her Ladies Auxiliary meetings. Fortunately, a visit from Mr. Wilcox in the cemetery had given her a chance to vent and get things off her chest. But before Mr. Wilcox could give her any sage advice, Becky was summoned by a voice she could hardly resist.

"Miss Becky!" Teeter hollered from the cemetery gate. "Miss Becky? You in there?"

"Hey, Teeter," Becky called back and waved as she walked to the little boy. "What you doin' a-howlin' like an old coon hound?"

"Miss Becky, there's a man come calling for you," Teeter said before he looked over his shoulder.

"A man? What's he look like?" Becky briefly

wondered if it was Adam. She hadn't seen him in a dog's age, and she wanted to talk to him. After the police station, she was sure he thought she was dizzy. But she thought he always knew that. Wasn't that one of the things he liked about her?

"He's tall and skinny, and his eyes go like this." Teeter bugged his eyes wide open and stared up at the trees, then down at the ground, and finally at Becky, who clapped her hand over her mouth and laughed.

"Oh no. That's the Heathcliff boy." Becky groaned. "Teeter, I'll give you a nickel if you promise not to tell Mama you found me. Can you keep it a secret?"

"I sure can, Miss Becky. I know lots of secrets. I won't tell a soul." Teeter crossed his heart.

"Besides, Miss Fanny can have him. I'm sure he'd just love to chew her ear off about his delicate stomach while she boasted about the escargot she ate in Paris." Becky laughed again. "Sounds like a match made in heaven."

"I don't know what you mean, Miss Becky. But if you say so," Teeter replied, looking carefully around the entrance of the graveyard.

"Are you sure you wouldn't like to come in here

and sit a spell with me?" Becky asked. "It's mighty hot, and the shade of these big trees is very nice."

"No, ma'am." Teeter shook his head.

"All right. Then why don't you take me to meet Herman and his family down by the creek?" Becky said. "We better do it lickety-split."

"That sounds like a great idea. But why do we have to do it so fast, Miss Becky?" Teeter asked, taking her hand once she left the cemetery grounds.

"Well, I want to meet all of them before they croak," Becky said, winking.

Teeter howled. "You are funny, Miss Becky!"

When they finally came wandering back to the house, Kitty was once again fit to be tied.

"Rebecca Madeline Mackenzie, where have you been?" her mother scolded.

Before she could say another word, Becky hurried Teeter into the kitchen to Lucretia. Becky knew the little gent would lie for her, but she didn't want him to. If anyone had to lie, she'd do it.

"I took Teeter down to the creek. You know he found that big frog, Herman, and I asked him to show me where. We looked for more, thinking maybe we could have frog legs for dinner as long as they weren't Herman's kin." Becky smiled.

"The Heathcliff boy paid a visit, looking for you."
Kitty huffed.

"I had no idea he was coming. Why, I haven't seen him in ages. I'm sure Fanny kept him entertained," Becky said, flipping her bobbed hair over her shoulder.

"Fanny had a headache. She went to lie down," Kitty said then pinched her lips together. "You know, if you just gave him a chance, I'll bet he's just as nice as that Northern boy you keep crooning over."

Becky looked down at her feet and then clasped her hands in front of her. "I'm not sure you've got anything to worry about with that Yankee, Mama." She felt a sting in her eyes but blinked the tears back quickly.

Before Kitty could ask her daughter anything more, Teddy came shuffling over from next door.

"Well, what a vision. Kitty, you do get prettier every time I stop by," he said, schmoozing. "Becky, just the dame I was looking for."

"Why, Theodore, does your mother know you're addressing the fine ladies of Savannah that way?" Becky teased.

Kitty left them on the porch, and Becky began to bounce on her heels.

"Please tell me there is something going on

tonight. I'm going batty in this house. I thought after Willie's and the police station that you guys were fed up with me," Becky said.

"Becky, we all know you're an odd duck. That's part of your charm," Teddy replied, clicking his tongue and winking. "And there is something going on, doll. A party to end all parties."

"I thought that was Martha's birthday party," Becky whispered.

"Why, Rebecca, you scamp," Teddy said out of the side of his mouth. "I'll pick you up at nine. And bring that dish of a cousin of yours."

"Oh, Teddy, do I have to?"

"Trust me. This party will be jumping so high she won't have time to bug you. I've got a buddy just back from Biloxi who is just her type." Teddy patted Becky's shoulder.

"Male? Brilliant, Sherlock." Becky shook her head and planted her hands on her hips.

"Trust me, Becky. Just be ready to scram at nine. I'll have the motor running." Teddy's eyebrows bounced.

CHAPTER TWENTY-THREE

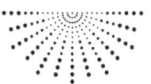

*B*ecky had decided she wouldn't spend any more time worrying about the dirty little hobo or Madame Cecelia or Adam or poor Lawrence Hoolihan. Instead, she slipped into her most daring dress, which was dark blue with purple beads. Even though she'd decided Madame Cecelia was off her rocker, she couldn't help but like the bracelet she'd given her.

"I'll just wear it this one last time and then bring it back," Becky muttered as she slipped it on. "I can't keep it. And if they are so interested in money, they can get a pretty penny for it." The bauble immediately snagged on her glove, but Becky carefully adjusted it and then admired her reflection in the mirror. Unless Cousin Fanny was wearing nothing at all, there was no way Becky was going to be concealed by her shadow tonight.

It was almost nine o'clock when Becky came downstairs and heard her parents in the parlor. They weren't arguing, but firm and precise words were being thrown around.

"We can let them both go out this evening, but tomorrow we'll have to talk to them," Judge said. "I'm as upset about this as you, but canceling their fun tonight would be unfair."

"Judge, do you really think the man responsible for the killing at the Bourdeauxs is hiding in Savannah? Maybe the police are wrong," Kitty fretted. Becky inched closer to the door and held her breath as she listened.

"That's what I heard from the boys at the barber shop this evening." Judge had gone into town, as he liked to do on occasion. He'd have a shave and a haircut then perhaps a quick snort of some bathtub gin from the back room before he sat down to hear the town gossip. He referred to what he'd gathered from the fellas.

"If they know that, why can't they go arrest him?" Kitty asked in her nervous, frail way. Becky knew her mother was looking at Judge with pleading eyes while wringing her hands.

"Now, Kitty, if they think this hoodlum is in town somewhere, they'll tighten the noose and squeeze him out in good time," Judge said soothingly. "Besides, he killed a man. It was in the most cowardly fashion of a knife in the back. However, the police don't believe he's out to harm any women. He might be just lying low until he can hop the next train to Mississippi or Chicago or who knows where."

"This is just terrible," Kitty muttered.

"Some of the folks think the Bourdeauxs know the culprit," Judge said as he cleared his throat. "That they might be hiding him. Protecting him."

Becky felt her stomach tighten. The Bourdeauxs were the kindest, sweetest people who ever lived. How could anyone say such trash?

"You don't think that's true, do you?" Kitty asked Judge.

"Course I don't."

"They've been through enough with all the stories flying around town about them since this happened. I was sure it was just some of the ladies at the boutiques spinning yarns to keep the customers entertained, but you say the men are saying it too?" Becky knew her mother was shaking her head even without looking at her.

"Poor Leona. I know this has got to be wearing her thin."

"Ha." Judge let out a good chuckle. "One thing about Leona Bourdeaux is she isn't afraid of what the townsfolk think. They may talk behind her back, but not a single one of them will utter anything disrespectful to her face."

That is true, Becky thought and was happy to hear her mother giggle a little at Judge's remark.

"You are right about that."

"Now, Kitty, we'll let the girls go out tonight, and we'll talk with them in the morning about what's being said. Am I correct?"

"Yes, Judge. That'll do."

Becky waited a couple of seconds before making a fuss as if she'd just come down the stairs and hadn't been eavesdropping on their conversation.

"My, oh my. You do look pretty tonight. Where is it that Teddy is taking you gals?" Judge asked.

"I don't know for sure," Becky said while she fidgeted with her gloves and inspected the contents of her clutch just as her bracelet snagged again. "He mentioned something about a friend of his just getting home for a week or so from Biloxi. Basic training, I suppose."

"Oh, now that does put my mind at ease that

you'll be with a man who can defend you if necessary," Kitty exclaimed.

"Teddy thought he'd be a perfect match for Fanny," Becky said, almost laughing as her mother's face fell. "Isn't that nice? I trust Teddy's judgment as much as my own. I bet there will be wedding bells before the month is out."

"Now, Becky, you quit teasing your mama," Judge said as he tried not to chuckle. He dug his thumb into his wife's side, making her squeal and laugh and then slap his strong arm.

"Behave yourself, Judge." She rolled her eyes and walked up to her daughter.

"Your hair looks real fine. That color makes the red just pop. Now, you be careful and stick with Teddy. Don't go off alone, and take Fanny with you to the ladies' room. There is safety in numbers."

"Ain't nothing going to happen to me, Mama. Besides, I hear the Heathcliff boy will be there. It'll be like I have a second shadow." She kissed Kitty on the cheek and walked to the door just as Teddy was pulling up.

Just then, Fanny came strolling down the stairs in a beautiful dress that Becky was sure she'd say she got in Paris.

"Why, Fanny, you look like a true Georgia peach," Kitty said.

"Thank you, Aunt Kitty. I got this dress in Paris and thought that exact thing when I saw it in one of the more upscale boutiques. I said to Granny Louise that I must have a dress the color of a Georgia peach. Why, we scooped it up immediately and—"

"And we're going to be late. Let's go. Night, Mama. Night, Daddy," Becky said as she hurried out the front screen door and let it slam shut on Fanny.

"Don't be too late!" Kitty waved as both girls piled into Teddy's car. "Teddy, you bring them home in one piece."

Teddy honked the horn before slipping the car into gear and driving off.

"So, where is this party tonight?" Becky asked.

"Near the docks downtown." Teddy lifted his chin as he spoke. "There is a row of apartments, and my good friend Lance decided to throw a rub in his new digs."

"Downtown?" Becky asked, remembering what she overheard her parents talking about.

"Well, kinda-sorta downtown. Look, it'll be a riot. Just trust me."

Becky thought Teddy looked like the cat that swallowed the canary. But she had always been up for an adventure. This was no different from the juice joint on the river or any speakeasy she slipped into. However, something in her gut made her feel uneasy. It had to be her parents' conversation and nothing more. They'd put a bee in her bonnet.

"And I think a certain fella from the papers is going to be there too," Teddy added.

Becky snapped her head around to stare at him, but he was not biting. Instead, he grinned and looked out at the road in front of them.

"Rebecca, I don't think your mother would approve of you seeing that boy. Especially when they are so worried about this situation with the Bourdeauxs' killer," Fanny piped up from the rumble seat.

"He's not the *Bourdeauxs'* killer, Fanny. It's not like they hired him to attend Martha's party." Becky knew full well why Fanny didn't want her seeing Adam. She wanted to sink her claws into him herself. And it made Becky rage inside that he didn't seem to do very much to discourage her from doing just that. All the worry about what her parents had discussed instantly left her. She scooted in her seat and took the cigarette that Teddy had just lit from his mouth. Then she took a puff before putting it back where she'd found it.

"I'm not saying that. I'm just saying that that sort

of thing is stressful enough, and you don't need to add to your mother's concerns by flirting with a boy who can only bring you misery." Fanny leaned over, letting Teddy get a healthy glimpse of cleavage that almost made him drive off the road. "Wouldn't you agree, Theodore?"

"Whatever you say, Fanny, my dear," Teddy replied after gaining control of the car again.

Becky was fit to be tied, so she kept her mouth shut for the rest of the ride, letting Fanny spin her web all around Teddy. She couldn't compete with all that. The best she could hope for was that sooner or later, everyone would see through Fanny's ruse.

Finally, they reached the place. It wasn't hard to find. The music from the apartment echoed down the street from two open windows. There were folks perched on the fire escape, and a few more had found a couple of dark corners where they had escaped for a few minutes to neck before going back to the party.

"Delilah? Zachary? Is that you?" Becky teased as she hopped out of the car.

"Hi, Becky," they replied in unison.

"I'm telling you, if I ever saw one of you without the other, I don't think I'd recognize who I was talking to. How's the digs?" Becky pointed up at the open window.

"Real nice," Zachary said.

"Tell it to Sweeney, Zach. You two probably haven't even made it up there yet. Would you like me to bring you a drink down so you don't have to stop what you're doing?" Becky smirked.

"We'll be up in no time." Delilah laughed.

"Sure. Sure."

Becky hurried up the stoop, which was also crowded with people, and said hello to several of them in passing. When she opened the door, the entire stairwell was crammed with people holding cigarettes and mason jars. Everyone looked like they were having fun, and Becky was ready to join them.

As she squeezed her way up the steps to the source of the music, she heard someone calling her name. She looked but couldn't see over the heads of all the people. With a shrug she went into the apartment, found the spare room that was really just a closet where the gin was being generously poured, took a jar for herself, and began to mingle. It didn't take long for her to find him.

Adam sat on a flimsy chair that looked barely strong enough to hold his big frame. He was looking right at her, his sleeves rolled up around his strong arms and his forehead wet with sweat. Inside the apartment, it was hot, but what Becky was feeling was something more.

But before she could pull up the courage to go talk to him, Fanny sauntered in. Like a magnet, she found Adam, who stood up and shook her hand. When he looked up, Becky made darn sure that he saw her turn and walk into the kitchen.

"There you are!" Martha shouted as she stuffed some kind of food into her mouth. "I've been waiting all night for you."

"I'm glad someone has." Becky sighed and joined her friend.

CHAPTER TWENTY-FOUR

"*W*hy, is that my favorite redhead?" asked a voice from a stove that radiated more heat than the street out front at noontime.

"Hank? What are you doing here?" Becky stepped up to him and peered over his shoulder at the skillet in his hand. "Willie's let you go?"

"No. Scheduled raid. Boss told all the regulars to take a hike while he handled the police. We'll be back in business in no time," he said while shaking what appeared to be sausage in the frying pan.

"I didn't know you could cook. Why, you'll make some lucky lady the most beautiful wife," Becky said, giving his beefy arm a squeeze.

"You try these sausages and peppers I'm making,

and I bet you'll have a ring for me by sunrise," Hank laughed.

"Since you aren't on guard, you want to cut the rug? I've never seen you dance before. I bet you're the bee's knees," Becky said. She wasn't serious with Hank. He had a reputation of being a real kneecap breaker. In fact, she was sure that was where he earned himself a few extra bucks. But she couldn't help but like him. Being friends with a guy his size was the next best thing to dating one. She was sure she wasn't the only lady happy a guy like him was around.

"I'm more like the bee's backside. But when you get hungry, come my way." He winked and clicked his tongue. "I'll save you a bite." Suddenly his eyes snapped to something behind Becky, and she saw him practically melt. "I see you brought trouble with you." Of course, he saw Teddy with Fanny.

"Ugh, you're on your own with that one, Hank. Be careful. The edges are sharp." Becky patted him on the back.

"They look smooth to me," he muttered before turning back to his skillet.

"I do not like how she constantly clings to Teddy," Martha said, crossing her legs and taking a sip from her own mason jar. "Tell me, Becks. Is she after him?"

"No more than she's after every other Johnny in the place," Becky said, hiding the twinge of pain in her heart. "She rushed up to Adam like he was a life preserver and she was drowning."

"Well, I can hardly blame the girl for that." Martha nudged Becky with her elbow. "Are you going to go talk to him? I know every time someone came through the door, he looked up. I'm pretty sure he was looking for you."

"If that's true, how come he didn't even get up when he saw me? And yes, he did see me just before Fanny filled up his line of vision." Becky shook her head, making her red curls bounce around her face. "Martha, am I normal?"

"Absolutely not." Martha smiled broadly. "That's why I love you. I know it's been hectic these past few weeks, and we haven't had nearly the right amount of visits we should have. But once things with… the murder," she whispered, "die down, everything will be back to normal, and you'll feel better. I'm sure that having Miss Fanny on your heels at home hasn't helped."

"Did I tell you she was snooping in my room?" Becky asked as she watched her cousin awkwardly try to do the foxtrot. "For someone who boasted about her trip to Paris, I have to ask, don't they dance there? She's two left feet and all wet."

Martha laughed, and then Becky laughed, and before they knew it, they were laughing at just about everything.

"Well, Leona, my mother, had Father Bartholomew come and bless the house again," Martha said, her words starting to slur slightly. "It was very nice. He walked through the whole house and blessed each room with a sprinkle of water. He even blessed the bar. And the jars of hooch in the basement. I think my daddy made sure he left with one."

"Well, that was mighty kind of your daddy," Becky said encouragingly. "He is nothing but one hundred percent pure Southern gentleman. Tell me, have the police told him anything about the murder? That he doesn't already know, having the crime committed in his own home and all."

Martha put her index finger to her lips. "I'm not supposed to talk about it. The ladies in town have been all over Mama for details. The ones that never had any time to speak to her before suddenly invite her for lemonade and pie. But my mama is smarter than all of them. She tells them she'd love to but can't because she's behind on alphabetizing her poisons and cleaning her rifles."

"She did not utter those words!" Becky howled, slapping the table.

"Sure did. I heard her myself say it to your favorite lady, Mrs. Heathcliff." Martha nodded her head all the way back and all the way forth until her chin touched her chest.

"Oh, that busybody." Becky blew a loud, juicy raspberry. "I just don't know why her son is fixed on me. I never said nothing out of the ordinary to him. Maybe I suggested he not take any wooden nickels. That's the best advice I could come up with, although he did give you a lovely present for your birthday."

"He did?"

"He gave you a thermometer. I thought that was rather clever," Becky said.

"That's funny. I don't remember. Everything kind of went hazy after… the incident." Martha frowned and squinted at the same time.

"What about you? Anyone giving you the bum's rush? I'll sic Hank on them," Becky said, taking a cigarette from the gent who squeezed into the kitchen next to her.

He lit it quickly, and after Becky took a puff, she

held it in Martha's mouth for her to do the same. Then Becky handed it back to the gent, who gave her a wink and thanks before heading back into the living room, where a lot of floor stomping was going on.

"None of the people that matter to me," Martha said. She'd hit her limit, and Becky saw the tears coming to her eyes. Leave it to Martha to be at the best party that had been thrown in weeks and get all bleary-eyed. "I know some of those debutantes are eating it up, thinking that I'm just staying in like a wallflower. But they ain't better than me. Or you. You're the cat's pajamas, Rebecca Madeline Mackenzie. You couldn't be sweeter to me than if you were my own sister. I'd be lost without you. Do you hear me? Lost."

"Hey, Hank!" Becky shouted over the music and the conversation. "How long until that grub is ready? Martha needs a little something in her stomach if she's going to last the night."

"Hot stuff coming up," Hank said and grabbed a saucer and loaded it with his sausage-and-peppers concoction. "You know who taught me how to make this? That sheik of yours. Adam What's-His-Name."

"He ain't my sheik," Becky snapped.

"He is so!" Martha piped up, the tears suddenly gone.

Becky took the plate and pushed it on Martha. "Here. Put something in your pie hole, please. I'm going to go get us a refill. I'm the Sahara Desert." Becky scooted out from behind the table. She didn't get five feet before Sam Lustyk scooped her up for a quick dance.

"That big palooka you're always eyeballing is making with the puppy dog eyes, Becks. It ain't none of my business, but are you guys on the outs?" Sam asked.

"It's complicated. Especially when a third gets added to what should have been a duo." Becky saw Fanny staring at Adam, and it made her miss her step. She landed squarely on Sam's toe. "Oh, I'm so sorry, Sam. I think I need another drink."

"Well, you get your sea legs and then come back to me, baby. The night is young." He stepped back, took Becky's hand, and kissed it.

"I'll do just that," Becky promised. Then she carefully wove her way through the room to the spare room where the booze was. When she emerged with a mason jar filled with ice and gin, she caught a glimpse of a peculiar feather poking straight up from someone's head.

Across the room, a tall man in a turban was pulling scarves from his sleeve to the bewilderment of a couple of ladies. He was Count Ernesto. Smirking, Becky was going to go say hello, but before she could squeeze through the crowd, she felt someone take hold of her hand.

The music changed to a slower song, and before Becky knew what was happening, she was in Adam's arms. After a few seconds and sips from her mason jar, he spoke.

"You didn't think you could avoid me all night, did you?" He stared down at her, his eyebrows arching up.

"Well, I figured you had your hands full with my cousin just pouring herself out in front of you," Becky said. "You didn't seem to mind being her knight in shining armor the other night. Remember? When you didn't believe me."

"First, Rebecca, I don't recall needing anyone's permission to get two ladies out of a dangerous situation." Becky tried to pull away from him, but Adam held her tighter. Her knees went rubbery, and she hated them for that. "Second, I didn't see some old ragamuffin coming out of the paddy wagon like you said you saw. What did you want me to do? Lie just so you'd feel better?"

Becky shrugged. "I wanted you to listen to me. Is your mother ill, Adam?" She felt a little lightheaded. The feeling swept over her like a breeze from a fan and then left just as quickly. But when her head cleared, she had a vision of an older lady who had wavy hair like Adam's lingering in her mind's eye. The woman was in bed, but she was smiling and alert.

His feet stopped moving. "She had a fever. Why? How do you know?"

"She's fine now. She's up in bed, and she's smiling. Ought to be her old self again in just a few more days. Doc will probably tell her to rest. You make sure she does." Becky blinked up at Adam. She waited for him to fling her aside, point at her, call her a con, or something worse. "I've been able to know things, see things for quite some time. My whole life, actually. So what do you think of that?"

"I don't know what to think of it," Adam said, his grip loosening.

Becky's heart sank to the floor, where she was sure it got smashed under the happy feet of those who jumped in as soon as the music picked up.

"Is it true you spend a lot of time in a cemetery that is on your property?"

Before Becky could feel sorry for herself, she felt

her blood boil. "So, you have been chatting with Fanny. How long did she wait to tell you what she thinks she knows about me?"

"Just calm down. I'm asking you a question," Adam said.

"If you'll excuse me, Mr. White, I do believe I need a little air. Thank you for the dance." Becky ripped away from Adam, spilling some of her drink on the floor. She wanted to go and divulge everything to Martha, but her body felt like it was going to burst into flames. Just a little cool air was all she needed. Without too much trouble, she wiggled out onto the fire escape. The cool city air was invigorating.

"What did I do?" she muttered. She took a seat on one of the rusty steps, pulled a cigarette from her clutch, and lit it. As much as she didn't want to, she had to go apologize to Adam. She'd spill the beans and come clean on everything, and either he'd accept it, or he wouldn't. It was that simple.

"He won't." The words came from behind her on the landing. When Becky turned around, she gasped. "He won't understand, and he won't want anything to do with you."

"Who *are* you?" Becky snapped at the familiar dirty face of the bum who had been showing up all over town wherever she was. "I'm not scared of you."

"Ha! Ha!" He pointed a dirty, crusty finger at her before slithering back into the apartment. "You'll be with me before long. Just like Lawrence Hoolihan. Just like Diggs. Just like so many of them."

Then he was gone. Becky tripped over herself dashing toward the window. She looked inside to see where the little monster had gone. But everyone was dancing and laughing and having a good time as if they hadn't seen anything. With all ladylike decorum thrown to the wind, Becky hustled back inside the hot apartment. Her eyes widened as she scanned the room.

"Where did he go?" she mumbled.

She could have shouted, but she doubted anyone would have heard her over the noise. The party was a real barnburner. She started to walk right through the dancers when she was yanked back. Her bracelet had snagged on the curtain. Part of her wanted to just rip it away. This was a bachelor place. A rip in the curtain would hardly be noticed. But her mama didn't raise her to abuse people's hospitality and cause damage to the home she was invited into. She shook her head, and her fingers fumbled, pulled, tugged, and stretched the fabric to get free from it.

Finally, the elegant little barbs let go, and she was released.

When she focused on the crowd of partygoers, she spotted the hobo shuffling through the crowd unnoticed. It was like he was nothing more than a shadow, a bit of smoke from a cigar wafting through air. But then he settled, stopping and stooping to whisper into the ear of someone Becky knew, someone who listened intently as if he were hearing the words of a close confidant. Before she could slip away to the safety of Martha's or Teddy's or Adam's side, she was quickly corralled by the boy she'd been avoiding for weeks.

CHAPTER TWENTY-FIVE

"*H*ello, Becky," the Heathcliff boy said. His eyes were rimmed red like someone who had tied one on a couple hours ago but was unwilling to succumb to sleep or a cup of strong black coffee.

"Hi." Becky had forgotten his first name again. "Who was that man talking to you? That little man?"

The Heathcliff boy shook his head. "What little man?"

"That gent who looks like a bum from skid row. He whispered to you. Just now. Just this very second. Who was he?"

The Heathcliff boy looked down at Becky. He was so tall and thin that Becky felt she was in the shade of a skinny tree.

"You always say the strangest things." He chuckled. "It is not a wonder people talk about you the way they do."

"What do you mean? What *what* little man? He was... hey, who talks about me?" Becky didn't mean to sound so vain. She knew darn well that people talked about her and not all the words were kind ones. But it slapped her into the real world and away from that ghoulish troll that had been popping up everywhere there was trouble. She could deal with people talking about her. She wasn't sure what she should do about this bum who only she could see.

"My mother thinks if we married, it would tame you. She thinks once you start having children you'll settle down." The Heathcliff boy inched closer, making Becky back up slightly.

"Married? Children? I do declare, Mr. Heathcliff, that you are jumping the gun a wee bit early, wouldn't you agree? Although I am flattered by your offer, I don't believe I'm ready for settling." Becky cleared her throat.

"Come with me for a moment." He took hold of Becky's wrist and squeezed it tightly as he pulled her through the crowd of dancing, laughing people.

"Excuse me?" She tried to pry her fingers underneath his and wrestle out of his grip, but it was useless. He was holding her tightly and had no intention of letting her go until he said what he wanted to say. "Why, Mr. Heathcliff, you see, Martha is half seas over. I think I better tend to her first." Becky didn't want to talk alone with the Heathcliff boy. Not now. Couldn't he tell by her expression that she was upset or at least distracted?

"If she's half in the bag, she won't be going anywhere," he insisted. "I paid you a visit the other day. I had hoped if you didn't suspect I was coming calling on you at the Mackenzie Plantation, I might catch you. Seems I was wrong."

"I'm so sorry about that. You see, I really don't have a very solid schedule. I just sort of go whichever way the wind takes me and…" She continued to try to pull out of his grip. The heat of the night and the room made her skin slick, but it was still no use trying to get out of his clutch.

The crazy thing was that no one seemed to notice her distress. She was sure she'd locked eyes with Sam Lustyk, and he just smiled and went back to his drink. Adam had his back to the crowd, but Fanny, obviously working him over, was directly in Becky's line of view—and yet she didn't even acknowledge her. That wasn't surprising.

"We need to talk somewhere quiet," the Heath-cliff boy said. Becky only heard his words. A thick, invisible blanket fell over the crowd around her along with the music, the laughter, and the chatter and clinking of bottles and glasses, muffling all the sound. "Tell me, would you have entertained Lawrence Hoolihan when he came calling?"

Becky shook her head. She didn't hear him right. She thought he said Lawrence Hoolihan. "What did you say?"

"He said he was going to go calling on you when I mentioned I'd seen you had arrived at Martha's party."

The Heathcliff boy led Becky out of the apart-ment and across the crowded landing to the stairs and pulled her up to the next landing. Fewer people were there, but Becky felt she wasn't entirely alone. She could scream if she had to. Enough people were around. When she scanned the place, she saw that no one was looking her way. They did see her, didn't they? They noticed the Heathcliff boy had pulled her by her arm down the hallway, didn't they? She couldn't be sure. Nothing seemed right, like a dream of a familiar place that suddenly became scary and unfamiliar.

"I have never spoken to Lawrence Hoolihan... er, eh... Mr. Heathcliff. I must say I don't know what you mean." She still couldn't remember his first name.

"You've danced with him. I've seen you. At Willie's about seven months ago." The Heathcliff boy scowled.

"Seven months ago? Did I? I must say that you have a better memory than me. I've danced with plenty of gents. I just can't keep track," Becky rambled. She couldn't figure out what his intention was. Even though his grip around her wrist was tight, she was sure he didn't want anything more than to talk with her. After all, the man was awkward and uncoordinated and had a mother who was as determined to get him married off as Kitty was to do the same to her.

"You admit to dancing with a lot of fellows, do you?" he asked as he pulled her up to the next landing.

There were no apartments on that floor. The landing led to the door that opened to the roof. Someone had propped it open with a brick. The air was cooler with a hint of tar on it from the roof. When Becky looked up into the darkness outside, she saw where that dirty hobo had gone. He was up at the top of the steps, looking down at her with a rotten grin and fiery eyes.

Becky tried to pull free, but the Heathcliff boy was pulling her toward him.

"Hey! What's this all about? Turn me loose, Mr. Heathcliff! Turn me loose this instant, or you'll be sorry!" she threatened without having any idea how to back up her threat.

Before she could say another word, the Heathcliff boy turned loose her wrist, grabbed her, and pushed her into the wall.

"Don't you understand I love you?" he hissed in her face.

His breath was hot and foul but not like he'd had too much to drink. No. His breath stank like someone who didn't take their hygiene very seriously. Like a bum. She looked at the open door and saw him laughing. That little monster was hysterical, clapping and bouncing in place as he licked his lips and squinted.

"This isn't how you treat someone you love." Becky hoped to appeal to the Heathcliff boy's sense of reason. But when she looked into his eyes, she saw there was nothing there to appeal to. He stared at her with that same hysterical grin as the hobo.

They were connected somehow, joined together diabolically.

"I've been pursuing you for ages, Becky. How can you not see? But you notice me now, don't you?"

"It's kind of hard not to." She winced.

"I tried to court you like a proper lady, but you're not really a proper lady, are you. No. You spend your days in a cemetery." He snickered like a boy who'd caught a glimpse of her garter belt.

"So I see Fanny has been talking to you too. Boy, that girl will stop at nothing to make sure my business is spread like strawberry preserves all over town." Becky took a deep breath. Her eyes narrowed, and she put her hands on her hips. "Why don't you just say what's on your mind, Mr. Heathcliff, and let's be done with it."

"I was hoping you'd say something like that." The Heathcliff boy leaned in to kiss her, but Becky quickly snapped her head back and gave him a quick slap. Sure, she wouldn't win any boxing titles with her mitts, but she got her point across.

"Look, fella, you've given me an earful. I'm not buying whatever you're selling, and if Fanny Doshoffer is telling you otherwise, you are going to learn the hard way that that ain't the kind of dame to get information from. Savvy?"

"Your cousin Fanny never said a word to me. In fact, she wasn't all that accommodating when I called on you. She didn't like that I gave her the brush-off."

"Well, there's one smart move," Becky huffed.

"You should realize, Becky, that I don't need anyone telling me anything. I know you. Better than you think. You spend your days in the boneyard, and then you spend your nights leading men on, like me." The Heathcliff boy began to tremble. "You would have seen Lawrence Hoolihan if he'd come calling. If he'd had a chance to come calling on you, you would have treated him right proper."

The sinister tone of the Heathcliff boy's voice made Becky's skin ripple with disgust. She didn't dare ask what he meant. She knew. And she was appalled.

"Your mama would wash your mouth out with soap if she heard you talking like that. If you keep beating your gums, someone is going to overhear you and clean your clock." Becky tried to be tough, but when the Heathcliff boy lurched at her and her back hit the wall, she felt all her bravery slip out of her.

She had nowhere to go. She wasn't strong enough to push past him. He didn't appear to be in any hurry to let her go. And the more Becky stared at him, the more she was convinced he *wouldn't* let her go. He'd brought her to this landing knowing no one had seen them slip out. The Heathcliff boy was utterly forgettable. No one ever noticed him. He barely spoke, and when he did, it was of no importance. That was how he could stick a knife in poor Lawrence Hoolihan's back and just slip out of the room completely invisible.

"She thinks you are a troubled girl. I think that is what I love about you most. Like me, you are different, and you know it. Rather than fight it and try to be like everyone else, you wear it like a badge of honor." He stared at her, clearly enjoying her discomfort. "I didn't want Lawrence Hoolihan or any other man getting in my way. I feel now is the time to get married. And I won't let you say no. You'll die if you have to. But unlike Lawrence, I'll make sure you feel no pain." His eyes watered as he held in his overwhelming emotions.

"You killed Lawrence. You stabbed him in the back," Becky stuttered.

"Isn't it wonderful, Becky? You know my secret." The Heathcliff boy smiled as tears of joy rolled down his cheeks. "You know all about it, but you won't whisper a word to anyone. You see how we are joined by this event? It's brought us a closeness that no husband or wife would ever dream of having."

"You're not hitting on all sixes," Becky muttered. "If you think I'm gonna be holding the bag for what you did to poor Lawrence, you've got more than a few screws loose."

She swallowed, but there was barely any spit there. Her mouth was dry, and the shadow of trouble she was in grew darker and darker. Someone had turned up the party's music, and everyone was cutting the rug. No one knew she was missing.

"Oh, I think you might reconsider that. That is, if you want that big palooka Adam White to make it through the night," the Heathcliff boy hissed. "I know you're sweet on him. But he'll be wearing a Chicago overcoat if he has to. And I'll tell you all about it, too. And you'll keep my secrets because that is what a good wife does. You might fight me at first, but you'll learn. There is Kitty and Judge and Fanny and even Martha and Teddy for me to use to help you learn your lesson. But you'll learn it."

Becky began to tremble. How had this happened? How did she get in a place where a killer had her pressed against the wall in a dirty stairwell and started ticking off the people he'd kill if she didn't marry him? And more importantly, how was she going to get away?

She looked around, but the Heathcliff boy's aura seemed to fill up her whole field of vision. Still at the door to the roof was the dirty little hobo, who was gnashing his teeth as he watched with sadistic pleasure while the Heathcliff boy terrified Becky.

The only way out had to be *through*. She took a deep breath and attempted to bolt past the Heathcliff boy. Faking a dash to the right, she suddenly went left and took two long strides across the landing. But not only was his tall, lanky body too long for her to escape, but his grasp was too strong. Just as she thought she dodged him, Becky felt his arm slip violently around her waist and hook her backward, knocking her off her feet. Her head hit the wall, and she saw stars seconds before the Heathcliff boy was on top of her.

Then she thought quickly. Her hands shot up, and the pretty bracelet from Ophelia that had snagged on everything from the second she slipped it on her wrist until now suddenly proved to be very useful.

"Argh!" the Heathcliff boy screamed as he covered his face. Becky realized that as she swung her hands up, the small barbs caught the skin of his face and gave it a hard, stinging tug from the right of his nose all the way to his ear.

He leaned back in pain, his left hand over his cheek as blood started to drip between his fingers. Becky thought she might have bought herself a few precious seconds to get away, but the thought was dashed as the Heathcliff boy clamped his left hand down around her throat.

"Oh, Becky. Why?" he muttered.

As he began to squeeze, Becky thrashed her legs. She scratched at his hand and kicked as hard as she could on the wooden floor. She clawed at his arm, but he was in a trance. He must have decided this was it and he was going to kill her.

"It didn't have to be this way. We could have held each other's secrets, and no one else would have had to get hurt."

Becky tried to scream but couldn't. Nor could she gasp for air. She couldn't breathe. Her heart began to pound in her ears. Her eyes burned as she stared at the Heathcliff boy. She opened and closed her mouth like a fish out of water and felt the overwhelming urge to cry.

When she looked toward the open rooftop door, she no longer saw the hobo there. She saw the dark sky and was sure she would become swept up in it any second. Her soul, on its way to heaven, would swim weightlessly past the buildings and mingle in the night sky with the stars and planets before she arrived at the pearly gates to get her final judgment. This was the end. Her mother would be so heartbroken.

This last thought forced tears from the corners of her eyes. But just before slipping off into oblivion, she saw two big hands land on the Heathcliff boy's shoulders and yank him backward. Free from his grasp, Becky kicked her feet and scrambled up the steps to the open door, gulping up as much of the cool nighttime air as she could. The coughs hurt her throat, but within seconds she could see clearly again and was breathing fast.

She turned to see Count Ernesto, his turban and tall feather remaining securely on his head as his fist flew into the Heathcliff boy's face, rendering him completely unconscious within seconds.

"Are you all right?" he asked Becky.

"Yes. I'll be okay. I could use a stiff drink, though," she said as she cried. "How did you know I was up here?"

"Madame Cecelia had a vision," he said, his green eyes twinkling from a halo of thick, long lashes. "I'm joking. Nothing so elaborate. I saw that filthy little devil you've been chasing. I followed him and found you."

"You can see him?" Becky sat up straight and took Count Ernesto's hand in hers. "I know Madame Cecelia told me who he was, but after... oh, I was so rude to her. She must hate me. I'm a real heel."

"On the contrary, Rebecca. She doesn't hate you at all. She's been so worried about you since you touched that Ouija board she's barely been able to sleep."

Becky looked down and saw the bracelet.

"Hot dawg! This piece of hardware saved my life!" Becky cried and held it up for Count Ernesto to see. "Ophelia gave it to me. Said to give it back when I was done using it. Can you believe it?"

"I can." Count Ernesto stood, his feather bending against the ceiling.

"Hey, how did you know I'd be at this party? There have got to be at least a hundred hops going on all over Savannah. How did you know to come to this one?" Becky put her hand to her throat and worried the tender spots where the Heathcliff boy had pressed his fingers.

"I saw it in a crystal ball." He helped her down to the landing and over to the steps. The Heathcliff boy lay unconscious on the floor, his right eye shiny with a bruise and a slight trickle of blood at the corner of his mouth where his teeth had cut his lip.

"Really?" Becky gasped.

"No. Not at all. Your friend Adam White and I work together. He invited me." Count Ernesto led Becky downstairs, where he quickly took charge and had the police called. The party cleared out fast, as no one wanted to get caught with the hooch, nor did anyone who had so much as a jaywalking citation want to see the police. The music stopped. People dropped their glasses. In an effort to make a quick getaway, some people even swarmed the fire escape. There, Becky saw the old hobo. He scowled at her as he backed out of the window, his blackened, stubby fingers clinging to the windowsill, his eyes burning with anger and his lips pulled down in a wrinkled, grimy sneer.

By the time they took the Heathcliff boy into custody, his spring was sprung. He had come to yelling and hollering that he was the fall guy for someone else as the police slipped the cuffs on. Since all the coppers in Savannah knew her daddy, there was little doubt to her story. Count Ernesto also gave his testimony. Even though the police didn't take kindly to any person hailing from another region of the world, they were satisfied that he was telling the truth too.

When they were finally allowed to leave the scene, Becky didn't know whether she wanted to laugh or cry. When she finally stepped out onto the street and saw Fanny in Adam's arms, holding him tightly and shaking her head, the decision between laughing and crying had been made for her.

CHAPTER TWENTY-SIX

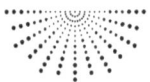

*a*lmost a month had passed since Neville Heathcliff had been taken into custody. As it turned out, he willingly confessed to killing poor Lawrence Hoolihan in a fit a jealousy and said he'd do it all again for the woman he loved. Fortunately, he didn't implicate Becky by name. He also confessed to killing a man by the name of Francis Diggs. When Becky read that in the paper, she nearly choked. But since the police hadn't said anything to her, apparently having forgotten about her paying them a visit the night Diggs was killed, she let that sleeping dog lie.

Martha and Teddy had come by several times in the interim and invited her to a slew of parties. But Becky just didn't have it in her. Something made her feel it was safer to stay close to home, at least for the time being.

"What are your plans today, sugar?" Judge asked his daughter as they sat around the breakfast table.

"I'm not sure. I think I'll see if Lucretia might teach me how to make a devil's food cake. Maybe," Becky said as she stirred a healthy helping of cream in her coffee. Strong black coffee brought back the memory of being in the diner with Adam. Becky wanted to erase that, so she did it with cream.

"Now, Becky, it isn't healthy for a girl your age to be holed up inside all day," Kitty urged. "I'd be happy to take you to town. Maybe you'd like to consider a new hairdo, or would you like to see if Gimbles's fall dresses are on display?"

"Not today, Mama. But thank you," Becky said.

"You are worrying me, gal." Kitty huffed as she spread a healthy pat of butter on her toast. "I don't think since you learned how to walk you ever spent so much time inside the house."

"Well, when my own mother tries to wed me to a murderer, that makes a girl reconsider her options," Becky said, lifting her chin.

Kitty gasped. "I did not try to wed you to a murderer." She looked at Judge, who laughed while hiding behind his newspaper, which rattled with every subtle shake of his body. "How can you let your daughter say such a thing? Judge?"

"It's all right, Mama. I forgive you," Becky said teasingly. "I knew you were desperate to marry me off. I just didn't realize how desperate you were."

"Had I known that the Heathcliff boy was capable of such horrors, I would have never even allowed him to set foot in my house," Kitty said. "Of course, his poor mother has to live with this shame. I do believe she is going to have to leave Savannah if she's going to have any kind of life at all."

"She should have left Savannah long before this." Judge chuckled. "She thought she had the goods on everyone in town. Turns out her own boy had her hoodwinked. I'm just very glad that my one and only child had the wits about her to fight back. I'm proud of you, sugar."

"I'd rather not talk about that anymore. It is obviously distressing Mama." Becky looked at her mother and smiled.

In truth, Becky herself didn't want to talk about it anymore. The incident had scared her more than she cared to admit. And even though she hadn't seen that horrible ragamuffin since he shimmied out the window, she had the feeling he was still out there somewhere, waiting for the chance to whisper in someone's ear and get them to do his nasty bidding.

She still didn't know exactly what he was or why just putting her hands on that Ouija board brought all this on her. She'd gone to the cemetery and talked with Mr. Wilcox and a few other of her spectral friends, but they had no answers either. Instead they spoke about their families in town or the work they had to finish. And Becky was ashamed to say she wasn't as interested as she once was in their tales. She felt she'd been robbed of something. The Heathcliff boy, Neville, hadn't taken anything from her. Instead, he'd given her something. A fear of her own gift. Something she'd grown up enjoying, even loving, had now become a facet she never wanted the sun to catch. That made her angrier than if he'd done what he had set out to do.

"Good mornin', y'all," Fanny said in a bubbly tone as she came into the dining room. "Oh, I slept so well. Aunt Kitty, I swear your down pillows are made from angel-wing feathers."

"Good morning, Fanny," Kitty said but looked at her daughter. "Fanny, I was trying to get my beautiful daughter out in the world today. Do you know of anything going on?"

"I'm afraid I don't," Fanny said without looking at

her cousin. Becky had gotten quite a bit of attention since *the incident*, and Fanny's trip to Paris had taken a back seat to it. "But I will say, Rebecca, that hanging around in the cemetery every day doesn't make you look any more sane than poor Mr. Heathcliff. I knew from the moment I met him that there was something peculiar going on inside his head."

"Of course you did," Becky replied.

"Becky, Cousin Fanny is only trying to help," Kitty interrupted.

"As I mentioned before, I was told that I have a keen sense of knowing the inner workings of people," Fanny boasted. "There was just something about the boy that gave me pause."

"Was it the fact that he turned down your advances?" Becky raised her eyebrows and pulled down her lips. "I'm sure that's never happened to you."

"Becky," Judge said in a low, firm voice.

"All I want is the best for you, Rebecca. I'm just glad that it's all over and life can go back to normal. When I was in Paris, I received some very valuable instruction from Grandma Louise, and it was that people will treat you exactly the way you let them. If you demand to be treated respectfully, then you will be. But if you don't demand it, you will be treated like the common riffraff." Fanny put an even healthier slab of butter on her toast than Kitty had and topped it with orange marmalade.

Becky took a sip of her coffee, hoping the hot liquid burning her tongue would distract her from the anger and jealousy she felt toward Fanny. She had no proof of it, but she was sure that the vamp was pursuing Adam. That was why she didn't mention going dancing at the Maharaja or playing cards at the juke joint down on the river. Those were just two of the invitations extended to Becky from Martha and Teddy, who said they'd told Fanny too.

"I'll take the rest of my coffee in my room," Becky said, shaking her head. She expected her mother to tell her to sit down, but the words never came.

"You'll never meet a new beau hiding in your room," Fanny said as Becky walked out of the dining room and into the kitchen to use the back stairs up to her room.

In Becky's mind flashed the image of her throwing the hot coffee in Fanny's face before grabbing her by the ear and twisting and tugging her to the front door, where she tossed her out. Instead, she took a deep breath, exhaled, and left the dining room.

"How could she even say that?" Becky muttered.

"She knows darn well that the only one I want is Adam. That's why Fanny sank her claws in him. He isn't rich, and he isn't well connected, but he is good looking, and he was mine. That was all the incentive Fanny needed to swoop right in."

Becky didn't know for a fact whether Adam had developed an itch for Fanny or not. She just assumed so after seeing him consoling her after the Heathcliff boy's attack.

"Ugh, they are right. I'm going to be fitted for a straitjacket and put in a padded cell if I don't get out of these digs," she muttered as she shut her door. Without leaving an opportunity to talk herself out of it, Becky got dressed, shimmied down the trellis, and headed over to Teddy's.

"Am I hallucinating?" Teddy quipped as he sat on the porch, sipping a mint julep. "Why... it is! Rebecca Mackenzie! I heard stories about you, but I didn't think you really existed. I'm so relieved you do."

"Cut the wisecracks. I need your jalopy," Becky said with a smirk.

"I think I know where you're going. Do you want some company?" Teddy asked as he pulled his keys from his pocket.

"No," Becky said without further explanation as she took the keys. "I'll try to bring it back in one piece." She leaned down and gave Teddy a kiss on the cheek.

"Martha is worried about you," Teddy added.

"Oh, tell her she doesn't have to worry. I'm fine, really," Becky lied.

"She's barely had anything to drink since that night. I've only seen her dance once. And I think if she has to sit and listen to Fanny talk about Paris one more time, there is going to be another murder," Teddy whispered the last two words of that sentence.

"Oh, well, then I'll have to lie low for one more night. Then you tell Martha to meet me at Willie's club. We'll have one last howdy-do and scram for parts unknown." Becky waved as she climbed into Teddy's car and sped off.

Like usual, it was jumping downtown. People were headed in every direction. No one looked at Becky or recognized her. She was just one of a million faces in town, and that made her feel good.

She knew where she wanted to go but wasn't sure what she would do when she got there. Her mind was going fast, yet her thoughts seemed reluctant to form, like rice pudding that hadn't sat long enough.

The sound of honking horns was soothing, and

the exhaust filtered through her nose but spread onto her taste buds, giving them a subtle smoky coating. Her hands sweated as she gripped the steering wheel, and she tried to think of something to say when she finally arrived at her destination.

"Oh, Becky, what are you fidgeting about? It's like you have ants in your pants," she scolded herself. "Just stop the car, get out, and go knock on the door and see what happens."

She couldn't wait any longer. Becky rounded one corner to the right then another to the left. Finally, she arrived at the skinny door and paced back and forth while she collected her thoughts. Ophelia opened the door. But before Becky could come up with anything witty to say, her eyes filled with tears, and she broke down into sobs.

"It's all right," Ophelia said as she pulled Becky to her. "You're safe here."

"I was so mean to Cecelia," Becky confided in the old woman. "I didn't want to listen to her. I was the epitome of bad manners. But had I done what she said, none of that would have happened, and—"

"And Neville Heathcliff would have gotten away with murder. Come. She's expecting you," Ophelia said.

"She is?"

"Of course." Ophelia chuckled, her one white eye staring blindly ahead while the other twinkled. "You have so much in common. So much to talk about. Go on up. You know the way."

Ophelia went back down to the store as Becky climbed the stairs, careful of all the statues and candles along the way. When she got to the top landing, she knocked on the door.

Footsteps could be heard running toward the door. Madame Cecelia flung it open, smiled as widely as ever, and gave Becky a big hug. "I'm so glad you are okay." She squeezed her tight.

"But I was so awful to you. I should have listened. I'm so sorry. Here." Becky pulled back and opened her clutch to retrieve the purple bangle bracelet. "You said to return it when I was done with it. I think it did what it was supposed to do."

"It sure did. Coffee? We have so much to talk about," Cecelia said.

"I'd love some," Becky replied. She already felt better.

ABOUT THE AUTHOR

Harper Lin is a *USA TODAY* bestselling cozy mystery author.

When she's not reading or writing, she loves hiking, doing yoga, and hanging out with her family and friends.

For a complete list of her books by series, visit her website.

www.HarperLin.com

www.ingramcontent.com/pod-product-compliance
Lightning Source LLC
Chambersburg PA
CBHW052017240626
47153CB00006B/1848